"Th... ...d
the... ...gue, and
all-around excellent storytelling. Every crime fan needs
to add the name Tom Piccirilli to his must-read list."
—Edgar- and Anthony-nominated author Victor Gischler

"Blackest noir, the most minimal kind of minimalism,
and at the same time deeply emotional: this is not
easy to do. I loved *The Cold Spot*." —Peter Abrahams,
bestselling author of *Nerve Damage*

"*The Cold Spot* is truly dazzling. Tom Piccirilli has
taken the mystery to a whole other level."
—Ken Bruen, Barry and Shamus Award–winning
author of *The Guards* and *American Skin*

"*The Cold Spot* is crime fiction at its very best, an ex-
ceptional revenge story so vivid you feel like you're
in the backseat of a getaway car with a master story-
teller at the wheel. If you like action-packed suspense
with serious bite, Tom Piccirilli is your man."
—Jason Starr, author of *The Follower*

"Tugged in by a stark, masterful setup, you'll stick
around eagerly for the knifelike prose, sharply
drawn characters and driving plotline. Lean, brutal
and completely arresting, Tom Piccirilli's *The Cold
Spot* is a bull's-eye hard-boiled tale." —Megan Abbott,
author of *Queenpin* and *The Song Is You*

"For all the violence and hard-boiled attitude, *The Cold Spot* has great heart. It also has a breakneck plot and a number of fascinating relationships. The ending anticipates a sequel. I can't wait to read it." —Ed Gorman, author of the Sam McCain series

"At the end of the book, several things remain unresolved, and there's plenty of room for a sequel or two. Because this book was so well done, so sharp, fast, and involving, I'm looking forward to reading them." —Bill Crider, author of the Sheriff Dan Rhodes series

Praise for Tom Piccirilli

"[Piccirilli] gives you the distinctive shiver . . . all good writing provides: the certainty that the writer's own ghosts are in it." —*New York Times Book Review*

"The gritty narration, graphic violence and pulp gravitas should make fans of Jim Thompson and Charlie Huston feel right at home." —*Kirkus Reviews*

"In a genre where twisted souls and violence are the norm, Piccirilli's work stands out for how it blends these elements with a literate sensibility." —*Publishers Weekly*

"Piccirilli is at the top of his game." —*Rocky Mountain News*

"Tom Piccirilli's fiction is visceral and unflinching, yet deeply insightful." —F. Paul Wilson, bestselling author of the Repairman Jack series

"Tom Piccirilli is a powerful, hard-hitting, fiercely original writer of suspense. I highly recommend him." —David Morrell, bestselling author of *Creepers* and *Scavenger*

THE COLD SPOT

SPOT

Tom Piccirilli

BANTAM BOOKS

THE COLD SPOT
A Bantam Book / May 2008

Published by Bantam Dell
A Division of Random House, Inc.
New York, New York

This is a work of fiction. Names, characters, places, and incidents
either are the product of the author's imagination or are used
fictitiously. Any resemblance to actual persons, living or dead,
events, or locales is entirely coincidental.

ISBN 978-0-553-59084-5

Printed in the United States of America
Published simultaneously in Canada

www.bantamdell.com

OPM   10 9 8 7 6 5 4 3 2 1

For Michelle

warm everywhere

and Ken Bruen

dark-hearted poet with soul ablaze

Special thanks to:

Duane Swierczynski, Allan Guthrie, Ray Banks, Jason Starr, Megan Abbott, Peter Abrahams, Ed Gorman, F. Paul Wilson, and David Morrell; Patrick Lussier and Matt Venne; RJ and Julia Sevin; and Dean Koontz.

Chuck Palahniuk, for the kind-of sorbet box of smells, sounds, and flavors.

My editor Caitlin Alexander, for her always eagle eye.

I hated what I had to do, but the devil drives.

—Ken Bruen, *The Killing of the Tinkers*

PART
1

Chase was laughing with the others during the poker game when his grandfather threw down his cards, took a deep pull on his beer, and with no expression at all shot Walcroft in the head.

Only Chase was startled. He leaped back in his seat knocking over some loose cash and an ashtray, the world tilting left while he went right. Jonah had palmed his .22 in his left hand and had it pressed to Walcroft's temple, a thin trail of smoke spiraling in the air and the smell of burning hair and skin wafting across the table into Chase's face.

You'd think it would be disgusting, acrid, but it was actually sort of fragrant. There was almost no blood. One small pop had filled the hotel room, quieter than striking a nail with a hammer. It didn't even frighten the pigeons off the sill.

Walcroft blinked twice, licked his lips, tried to

rise, and fell over backward as the slug rattled around inside his skull scrambling his brains. The whites of his eyes turned a bright, glistening red as he lay there clawing at the rug, twitching.

The others were already in motion. Chase saw it had been set up in advance, well planned, but nobody had let him in on it. They didn't entirely trust him. Jonah opened the closet door while Grayson and Rook lifted Walcroft's body and carried it across the room. Walcroft was trying to talk, a strange sound coming from far back in his throat. He was blinking, trying to focus his gaze, his hands still trembling.

Chase thought, He's staring at me.

They tossed Walcroft in the corner of the empty closet, slammed the door, and immediately began cleaning the place.

No one looked at Chase, which meant everybody was looking at him. Nobody said anything as they wiped down the room. So that was how it was going to be.

The room continued leaning and Chase had to angle his chin so things would straighten out. He shuddered once but covered it pretty well by bending and picking up the ashtray. They wouldn't want the butts tossed in the trash, they contained DNA. Maybe. Who the fuck knew. They were evidence anyway, some keen cop might nail Rook because he always tore the filter off his Camels. It was a clue.

Chase carefully split the cotton nubs apart, stepped to the bathroom, and threw them in the toilet. He washed out the ashtray. Maybe it was the right thing to do, maybe not. It could be downright stupid. It felt insane. What really mattered was they had to see he was trying, that he was very much a part of the crew.

He dove for the cold spot deep inside himself and seemed to miss it. He couldn't look at his face in the mirror. His heart slammed at his ribs, trying to squeeze through. He noticed he wasn't breathing through his nose, was beginning to pant. He started again. He made sure he left no prints on the toilet handle or around the sink. He tried to move into that place again and this time felt himself begin to freeze and harden.

When he got out of the bathroom the closet door was open a crack. Walcroft was still squirming and had kicked it back open. One shoe had come off and a folded hundred-dollar bill had fallen out. Rook said, "Son of a bitch," grabbed a pillow off one of the beds, and drew his .38. Walcroft kept making the sound.

Chase knew then he would hear it for years to come, in the harbor of his worst nightmares, and that when his own loneliest moment in the world came to pass he'd be doing the same thing, making that same noise. Rook stepped into the closet, stuffed the pillow down on Walcroft's face to stifle the shot, and pulled the trigger. There was a loud cough and a short burst of flame. This time the pigeons flew off. With his teeth clenched, Rook tamped out the pillowcase. He nabbed the c-note and shut the door again. That was finally the end of it.

Chase was fifteen and he'd been pulling scores with his grandfather for almost five years. First as a kid running two- and three-man grifts, a few short cons, kitten burglaries—as Walcroft had called them—and then working his way up to taking part in an occasional heist. Jonah always packed guns during jobs. Chase knew his grandfather had blasted his way out of a few tight situations, but so far he'd never seen Jonah kill a man.

Now this, one of his own crew, a part of his own string.

Earlier that day, the score had gone down smooth as newborn ass. They hit a bookie joint run out the back of a fish market owned by the North Jersey mob. Jonah had explained how years ago nobody would've dared mess with any of the syndicates, but the days of the mob families' real power were long over. They squabbled among themselves more than they battled the FBI. Sons put their fathers under. Wives turned informant on their Mafia boss husbands. Everybody flipped eventually.

So the four of them went after the book. It was sometimes a little tough putting the string together because a lot of pros wouldn't work with someone named Jonah, despite his first-rate rep. It was one of the reasons why Chase started as a driver so early on, just so they wouldn't need to find the extra guy. Besides, Jonah couldn't drive for shit.

Chase sat behind the wheel of a stolen '72 Chevy Nova that he'd tuned on his own. He'd also done the body work and new paint job. A Turbo 350 transmission, 454 bored engine, solid-lift camshaft, and a Flowmaster 3 exhaust so the car practically hummed like a struck chord. The horsepower seeped into his chest.

Part of being a wheelman was putting everything you had into a car and then letting it go again. After the heist they'd be able to sell it to a local chop shop for an extra ten grand, which Chase'd keep himself. For what Jonah called his college fund. It was a joke to all the crews they ran with, how young he was. It took a while but eventually they came to respect him. For his scouting and driving skills, his nerves, and the way he kept his mouth shut.

Rook and Grayson came out of the fish market with a sack of cash each. Jonah followed, carrying another two. Five seconds later Walcroft came prancing out the door holding a giant yellowfin tuna, smiling widely so that all you saw were his bright eyes and perfect teeth under the ski mask. It got Chase laughing.

They'd expected forty grand, maybe a little more since the fish market was the hub for six different books who all turned in their receipts on Friday noon, in time to get to the bank before the midday rush. Not a major score, but an easy one to keep them afloat until the next big thing came along.

They climbed into the Nova, Walcroft hugging the fish to him for another second and saying, "I shall miss you, my friend, but now, back to the smelly depths of Joisey with you," then tossing it in the parking lot. Chase let out a chuckle and eased down on the throttle, moving smoothly out of there.

They had a hotel room on the Lower West Side of Manhattan. Chase had the way perfectly mapped, the streetlights timed, and hit the road heading east just as some of the mob boys came running outside. One of the fat ginzos tripped over the fish and took a header. Both Chase and Walcroft started laughing harder.

The goombahs rushed for their Acuras and Tauruses. Nobody had too nice a car in case the IRS was watching. They followed the Nova for about a mile until Chase made a left turn from the right lane and bolted through a stale yellow light.

This was a family town. The mob mooks had grandchildren going to the school on the corner, their family priests were in the crosswalk heading to the local rectory. The Mafia gave it up with hardly a fight, too worried about running over a nun or crossing guard. It almost made Chase a little maudlin, thinking these guys had a home they cared for more than they did their own cash. He hadn't stayed in the same town for more than three months since he was ten years old.

He'd been ahead almost 150 bucks in the poker game. Walcroft about the same. Now Chase realized the others had let them win to distract them. He wondered if he'd been a little sharper and seen Jonah palming the gun, and had dared to warn Walcroft, would his grandfather have shot him in the head too.

Rook and Grayson finished wiping the room. There hadn't been that much to do, they'd been playing cards for less than an hour. They took their split of the score and said nothing to Chase, which meant they were saying a lot.

He listened to their footsteps recede down the hall and then sat back in his chair. Icy sweat burst across his forehead and prickled his scalp. He stared at the closet.

Chase had liked Walcroft. The man had taught Chase a little about computerized engines and how to circumvent the LoJack and other GPS tracking systems. Unlike all of Jonah's other cronies who'd bothered to teach Chase anything, Walcroft was young, only about twenty-five, and knew about the modern systems. The other pros and wheelmen were Jonah's age. They'd been at it for decades and only wanted to steal cars that came off the line pre-1970 because they were simpler to boost and reminded them of their youth.

A surge of nausea hit Chase like a fist. He wanted a bite of something but all the liquor bottles were gone. He spread his hands across the table and held himself in place until his stomach stopped rolling.

"Wipe that table down again," Jonah said. There was no heat in his steel-gray eyes, no ice.

A confidence man knew how to read human nature. He could see down through the gulf of complex emotion and know what people were feeling, which way they were likely to jump. Chase had gotten pretty good at it over the last few years on the grift.

At least he'd thought so. Now he looked at Jonah and tried to read him. He couldn't. There were no signs. Nothing but the hardness of stone.

Jonah stood five-nine, about two-twenty of rigid muscle, powerfully built. Fifty-five years old, compact, everything coiled, always giving off intense vibes. Mostly white hair buzzed down into a crew cut, just a flicker of silver on top. Huge forearms with some faded prison tats almost entirely covered by matted black hair.

There was a quiet but overpowering sense of danger to him, like he'd always speak softly and be perfectly calm even while he was kicking your teeth out. You knew if you ever took a run at him you'd have to kill him before he'd quit the fight. If he lost and you left him alive, he'd catch up with you at the end of an empty desert highway, barefoot on melting asphalt if he had to. You'd never stop looking over your shoulder. He'd mastered the ability of letting you know all this in the first three seconds after you met him. Nobody ever fucked with Jonah.

Now that lethal cool was filling the room. Chase had always thought it was directed at the other thugs and never at him, but here it was, turned all the way up, Jonah just watching.

So now Chase knew.

One wrong move and he'd be quivering in the closet. He met his grandfather's eyes and held firm, as rigid as he could be.

"I liked him," Chase said. "Tell me it wasn't because of the fish. You didn't snuff him because he was dancing around with the goddamn fish."

"He was wired," Jonah said.

"What? For who?"

"Who knows?"

Chase shook his head but didn't shift his gaze. "No. No way."

"It's true."

"I didn't see a wire."

"Even so."

There was nowhere else to go with it now.

Chase stood and started to make his way to the closet. Jonah blocked him and said, "We need to leave."

"We were going to stay here for three days."

"We've got another job waiting to be cased. We have to be in Baltimore by midnight."

"I want to see it."

"We don't have time for this. We need to go. Now."

Unable to do anything but repeat himself, like a brat demanding presents. "I want to see it."

"Rook took the tape and microphone."

"I didn't see him do that either."

"You were too busy trying not to throw up."

Said in the same flat tone as everything else Jonah ever said, but somehow there was still a hint of insult in it.

"Walcroft's chest will be shaved."

"It wasn't on his chest. It was down his pants."

"Then his goddamn pubes will be shaved."

Jonah crowded him now, refusing to get out of the way.

Had this been coming for a while? Chase wouldn't have thought so twenty minutes ago but abruptly he felt a fury asserting itself within him. As if this was the natural course for him and his grandfather to follow, the only one, and always had been. The two of them standing here together face-to-face with a dead man in the closet.

The air thickened with potential violence. Chase glanced down at Jonah's hand to see if he was still palming the .22. Jonah had his hand cupped to the side of his leg. Jesus Christ, he was. It had really come down to this.

Time to let it go, but Chase couldn't seem to do so. It was stupid, he could sense Jonah's thin patience about to snap, but maybe that's what he wanted. He wondered if his need to push the

wood recycled into new use

Drop your mattress off for fr

of our collection sites.

There's free m

Visit **ByeByeMattre**

point had anything to do with his parents, with the way his father had ended up.

"Why would Walcroft suddenly start wearing a wire?" Chase asked.

"You say that like it's an actual question."

Maybe it wasn't. Everybody eventually flipped. Chase moved another step forward so that their chests nearly touched. He realized there was no way he could beat Jonah, but at least the man would have to work a little harder for it than a quick tap to the temple. All these years, all the talk about blood and family, of fatherhood and childhood, the discussions about unfulfilled vengeance, going after his mother's killer, and they'd come down to this. Two kids in a sandbox.

"Why did you really ace him?"

"We need to leave."

"You didn't even blink," Chase said. "You've done it before."

"You asking for any special reason?"

"I'm not asking. I can see it now. You've done it before."

"Only when I had to."

"You didn't even let me in on it."

"Would you have wanted to be?"

Probably not but what was he going to say? "What if I'd hesitated? Those two would have killed me too."

"There was no chance of you hesitating. I taught you better than that. You're a pro."

It was a comment meant to appeal to Chase's

vanity. There was no substance or emotion behind it. Jonah didn't quite understand how regular people felt about things, and when he tried to play to any kind of sentiment he always wound up way off base.

"I'm through," Chase said.

"You're not through."

"I'm going my own way."

"Turning your back on blood?"

"No," Chase told him. "You ever need me for something other than a score, let me know. I'll be there."

That almost made Jonah smile, except he didn't know how to do that either. "Going to start doing scores on your own? More second-story kitten burglaries, shinnying up the drainpipe? Knock over liquor stores and gas stations? Home invasions? You'll get picked up on your first run."

"A minute ago I was a pro."

Jonah stared at him, eyes empty of everything. You looked into them for too long and it would drive you straight out of your skull. "You're a string man now. You're part of a chain. You're a driver. You going to start working for other crews?"

"I don't know. Maybe I'll retire."

"And deliver newspapers?"

Jonah reached out and gripped Chase's arm, digging his fingers in deep. It hurt like hell. In the past two years Chase had grown to six feet and gained thirty pounds of muscle, but he knew he wasn't as icy as his grandfather. He didn't think he ever would be. He wondered for perhaps the ten thousandth time how his fatally weak father could have come from this man. Chase fought to remain expressionless.

His mind squirmed and buzzed with all his failed tasks and unaccomplished dreams. He hadn't yet killed the man who'd murdered his mother. He'd never made a major score.

"I don't have any answers," Chase admitted. "I just know we're through after this." He tried to shrug free but couldn't break his grandfather's hold. "Walcroft wasn't even dead yet."

"Close enough."

When you've got nowhere to go you go back to the beginning. "I didn't see a wire. I don't believe it."

"You've got an overabundance of faith."

"Not anymore. Let me go."

"Okay, then try it on your own," Jonah said, releasing him. "But wipe the table again before you do. You know how to get in touch with me if you need to."

They each packed their belongings and took their shares and split up as they moved down the hall. Jonah hit the button for the elevator and Chase hit the stairway. Fourteen floors, he wasn't going to beat Jonah to the ground, but he didn't want to be in a confined space with the man. When he came out he searched the lobby and didn't see any of the crew. He rushed out the door and down the block, still trying to take it all in. Got to the garage where

the Nova was parked but couldn't force himself inside it. He had to know.

Chase ran around the block back toward the
hotel. They'd forgotten or didn't care that he had
one of the room's two plastic card keys. He in-
tended to check Walcroft's body to see if he'd
really been wired.

A confidence man knew how to read human
nature. He could see down through the gulf of
complex emotion and know what people were
feeling, even if he didn't have those feelings himself.

Jonah had known he'd try it. His grandfather
stood on the opposite side of the block, perched
just inside a storefront. He was wearing a jacket,
his arms crossed against his chest. That meant the
.22 was back in its ankle holster and his .38 was on
his belt, and his knife was at the small of his back.

Look at this shit, the things you've got to worry
about now. Like wondering if Jonah or one of the
others might tip the cops about the Nova. Was it
possible? The fish-market goombahs wouldn't have
called the police so the car should still be clean
enough to get out of New York. Unless Jonah had
given Chase up directly to the mob, told the fish-
market guys, Hey, you want some of your cash
back, this kid right here has it.

His grandfather might ace him but would he
turn rat? Chase couldn't see it but he couldn't see
Jonah snuffing Walcroft until he'd done it.

No, the Chevy Nova he'd rebuilt from the tires up was out now.

Chase moved past the garage and caught a bus at the corner heading crosstown. He didn't feel any fear or hope or excitement. He'd shifted gears again and now his life was on a different road.

*F*ive months later Chase was stealing cars for a Jersey chop shop run by a small-time Mafia bagman called the Deuce.

Deuce had a scam going where he'd strip sports cars and dump the frames back onto the street, wait for the insurance companies to auction them off, buy them up for just a couple of bucks, then reassemble the cars with the original parts and sell them legally to the crime families. He was known as Uncle Deucie to all the Mafia princesses driving around in the Ferraris and Porsches he'd sold them for a flash of leg. All day long the Deuce would be on the phone promising the little darlings anything they might want for Christmas or their birthdays or when they graduated high school. He liked the attention but never let it go any further than that for fear some mob torpedo would punch his ticket for crossing a line.

Tuned in to an oldies station—the vibrant and charged black female harmonies working through his guts like the thrum of the engine—Chase slid into the garage driving a Mercedes SUV, sort of grooving in his seat.

He'd boosted the truck from a high-end dance club on the shore known for its coke trade, where the valet parkers and the bouncers always left the front door uncovered around closing because they were off getting blowjobs in the little security booth. The locked glove box held an envelope with twenty-four hundred bucks cash, a fifth of Cuervo, and a few tabs of acid. Owner was probably a rich dude turned small-time hustler, who brought drunk Jersey City high-hair chicks out to the truck and banged them in the backseat.

Chase had pocketed the money and tequila and tossed the LSD out the window. It was now 3:00 A.M., the slowest time for the shop. He parked in a stall and shut his eyes, swaying and tapping the shift knob while the song finished.

It was rare but, on occasion, usually in the dark of predawn with a suggestion of rain in the air, he could manage to drift from himself just far enough to start thinking about what his next step should be.

Tugging the wires in the cracked steering column apart, he listened to the echoes of the engine stalling across the bay. The place was empty except for a couple of Puerto Rican guys arguing in Spanish and trying to wrestle loose the transmission from a Jaguar. They'd never worked on one before and were perplexed by the layout. Chase didn't know much about Jags either. He'd just decided to help out and learn whatever he could when the Deuce stepped over, opened his pocketknife, and started cleaning his fingernails.

Deuce said, "Heard about your gramps."

Now what. Now what the fuck what.

Already sensing he was going to have to cut and run tonight, Chase prepared to make a move. He hoped to Christ this had nothing to do with the mob finding out about the fish-market boost. You never knew when something was going to roll back onto you. He had almost twenty-two grand stashed in a bank deposit box he'd rented with some fake ID and wondered if he'd be able to hold out until morning and go back for it.

"Heard what?" Chase asked.

"Him and Rook and Buzzard Allen were holed up in a museum down in Philly last night. They were going after some Renaissance paintings and rare coins, who the hell knows what fence they got. Only one I know who can move that kind of product is Joe Timpo, and he's doing ten in Attica. Maybe nine. Nine or ten. Renaissance paintings, the hell is that? Who's gonna hang any of that in their living rooms, even the private collectors they got today? Rare coins, sixteenth-century, Spanish I think. Spanish or Italian. Or Portuguese."

"Back to Jonah," Chase said, checking the door, the guys working the Jag. If this was a setup, it was a slow one.

Deuce put the knife away, pulled a half-smoked cigar out of his shirt pocket, and began chewing the end of it, a sure sign his tumblers were turning, trying to slip into place. "One of them blew away a cop and then started in on the hostages. Killed a security guard so they'd get a chopper. A fuckin' chopper. Where'd they think they were going? How do you escape in a helicopter, the thing zipping around in the air, buzzing Ben Franklin's grave, spooking everybody looking at the Liberty Bell? There's room for what, two or three people in that. Where they gonna fit the paintings? You use a chopper to get out of Hanoi, not fuckin' Philly."

"Must've been Buzzard."

"I don't know him."

"Me neither," Chase said, "but the other two aren't stupid."

"Well, they left Buzzard there with his brains leaking out his eye sockets, so I guess they didn't want him around their necks." Deucie grinned a little and paused, thinking he was clever with that line, a sterling wit making the stretch between buzzards and albatrosses. When he saw he wasn't going to get any acknowledgment, his smile collapsed and he went on. "Popped him and managed to punch a hole before too many police barricades and roadblocks were laid out and made a run in a getaway car. That's all I know."

"Philly's a tight city," Chase said. It was like trying to pull a heist in midtown Manhattan. Crammed streets, a red light at every corner, only

a couple of ways in and out. Rare coins and
Renaissance paintings? The hell was going on?
"Cops have their names and faces?"

"No."

"So how do you know it was Jonah and Rook
with this Buzzard guy?"

"That's what everybody's saying anyway, so
somebody spilled. Maybe Buzzard's pals are a little
steamed about what happened to him. You know
me, I spend my day on the phone, the line's always
humming." Deuce dug around in his pockets trying to come up with his Zippo, even though he'd
never light the cigar tip in the garage. "A lot of
these solo players, even the solid pros, they got
crazy superstitions. They don't like working a heist
with someone named Jonah."

"I know."

"And besides"— Deucie found the Zippo,
flipped the lid, sparked it, and then put it back
again leaving the cigar unlit—"a lot of people were
friends with Walcroft. He was popular, depend-
able, fun in the downtime. They didn't like how he
ended up."

Chase shouldn't say anything. Walcroft's sound
swept through him, the man's blazing red eyes
searching him out, even now. He fought for some
kind of reply, but whatever he came out with
would be totally wrong, there was no chance of
otherwise. How aggravating to feel a flush of hu-
miliation and anger rising up his neck and realize

he could only react defensively, despite all that had gone down. "Jonah said he was wired."

Deuce shrugged and nodded, his chin bobbing all over the place. "Maybe. Maybe. Yeah. It does happen. It certainly does." Saying it like it never happened.

"*¡Maricon!*" one of the Puerto Ricans shouted, and Chase spun, ready to fight or run. But the guy was just shouting because he couldn't get the headers of the Jag out and had skinned his knuckles with a socket extension.

"What time did this score go down?" Chase asked.

Deuce realized he'd chewed the cigar butt into tobacco chaw and spit it in the corner. "Eight last night, as the museum was closing."

There it was, the end of this road. Chase walked away while Deuce called after him, "Hey, where you going? Come on back, I need to pay you for the Mercedes."

Uh-huh. Chase got into his own car—a '68 GTO, primed and touched up but not yet fully repainted— and pulled out, knowing his time here was done. Even in the bent life stigma followed. Betraying one of your own crew, butchering hostages, wasting cops—it all brought down serious heat. Jonah and Rook were going to say Buzzard did it and every other pro would have to accept it even if they didn't believe it. That or go up against them. The whole mess might never be sorted out. No one would want to help Jonah for a while, and anybody hoping to cash in on a quick reward or plea bargain would blow the whistle. The cops would be beating the brush and back alleys trying to shake any bit of info out. A lot of deals were about to be cut.

Seven hours had gone by since Jonah's name had started getting kicked around again. Chase would have to leave the cache in the bank deposit box. He couldn't wait the extra day, too many people knew where he was. If there was a bounty put out on Jonah by Buzzard's friends, Deucie might turn Chase in himself, hoping he could lead them to his grandfather. You never knew. Chase didn't blame the Deuce, it was business.

He rushed back to his rented room with the driver's window down, letting the Jersey breeze wash over him, breathing it in deeply. It had a different kind of odor from anyplace else he'd ever been—full of pollution and pine, money and sex and corruption and action. It'd be the last time he smelled it for a while.

At the apartment he packed up, rolled the twenty-four hundred in with the three g's stashed in the spare tire, and drove west for five hours until he'd crossed into Ohio. On the way he drank nearly all the Cuervo. His stomach burned and so did the back of his skull.

He got a room at a cheap motel, but, exhausted as he was, he couldn't sleep. In ten days he'd turn sixteen. He put a couple of quarters in the bed and got the magic fingers going. It felt more like there was a bunch of chubby kids hiding under the bed poking him in the back.

The story continued to break fresh and wide on cable news. He watched the amateur footage of the standoff outside the museum in Philadelphia. It lasted only a few minutes before the robbers burst out of the place and made their run. The sound of gunshots and bullhorns scared the amateur into dropping his camcorder.

When Chase heard the hot Asian correspondent say that the driver had broken through the roadblock and nearly clipped a teenage tourist visiting with her history class for the weekend, Chase knew that Jonah'd had trouble putting together a new string. This time there'd been no driver and his grandfather had been forced to double as the wheelman himself.

They interviewed the girl while her friends mugged and hooted for the camera.

But she was dead-eyed and mechanical in her answers, pretty but stiff with ashen blurs already appearing under her eyes. She understood now just how close she'd come to wiping out of the game and being left shattered in the street without any reason, thought, or mercy.

*D*espite *the goofiness with the chopper and all the* rest of it, Jonah was back pulling notable scores within a year. Chase had been worried for the first few months after the botched museum heist so he kept in touch with Murphy, an old-time safecracker who'd done a nine count in the pen, took a bullet in the hip during his last job, and decided to retire. Now Murphy ran a used car lot in Fort Wayne, Indiana, with his two adult sons, and passed messages for the pros. He sold cars with clean papers to crews operating in the Midwest, and he always kept an ear out for any buzz or action.

Chase checked in a few times to find out what the word was on Jonah. It had taken a while for the stigma to fall away but eventually everybody just blamed Buzzard Allen for the troubles during the museum heist. Buzzard's friends apparently didn't like him enough to argue the point too emphatically.

Murphy asked, "You want me to give your grandfather a message?"

"No," Chase said and got on with his life.

For three years he worked his way mostly south under different names, stealing cars or driving getaway on various easy jobs. He stayed out of the circuit he had known and wound up in Tennessee running moonshine for a couple of months, listening to the locals talk about the federal government like they thought Lincoln was still in charge. Every time someone mentioned revenuers he'd burst out laughing. He couldn't help himself. He hadn't realized they really said shit like that.

They started acting like he might be undercover for the Treasury Department and he finally took off.

He met Lila while he was driving for a four-man string knocking over jewelry stores in northern Mississippi. They were a flashy bunch who liked to blow up gas stations for diversions. Nobody had died yet but that was bound to change. When Chase came on board for the job he talked them down from TNT to simply planting homemade smoke bombs in the kitchen of the one fairly upscale hotel in town. Same effect—a lot of confusion—but no one would get hurt.

They liked to argue among themselves and draw little diagrams and math equations with graphs and vectors before they decided on any move at all. It

made them feel smart. You'd think with all the nota-
tions and planning one of them might've brought
a flashlight, but the first thing they did when they
got inside Bookatee's Antiques & Rustic Curio
Emporium (Gold, Silver & Jewelry) was pull up the
shade to get some street light in the place.

Chase knew this crew wasn't going to last long,
but he'd recently lost a bank account of stashed
funds when the guy he'd bought his fake identifi-
cation from went down in a federal sting. The
name was useless now and the money had gone
with it. He needed to rebuild a quick cache.
Otherwise he'd never have worked with these
nitwits in the first place.

The crew assured him that Bookatee had
money and knew jewelry. This was where you
came for the good merchandise. So at midnight
Chase waited down the block in a '69 Mustang with
the lights off while the others boosted the goods.
He'd rebuilt the Mustang's engine from damn
near scratch and it hummed perfectly in tune with
the crickets and katydids, so that he could feel the
darkness throbbing. Sirens erupted in the distance. The fire engine was actually *clanging* on its
way to the scene. He looked over his shoulder
through the back window and watched a bloom of
smoke rise against the silver-tinged clouds.

It was only because he was glancing in that direction that he spotted the police cruiser easing
around the corner behind him. Mostly hidden in
the shadows of a large maple, he slid lower in his

seat. It was a warm night and hopefully the cop wouldn't spot the muffler vapor. The driver slowed in the middle of the road, then veered to the curb ahead of him. Chase cursed beneath his breath. A female deputy sheriff climbed out and craned her neck. She'd noticed Bookatee's window shade.

He sat up and drummed his fingers along the top of the steering wheel. She was pretty as hell and her body language somehow got to him—how she moved with poise and a solid, confident power. She stood at the outer rim of the streetlamp's circle of illumination. Why wasn't she calling it in yet, asking for backup? Probably because she didn't want to pull anybody off the fire detail where they might be needed.

Chase noted her full lips, dark eyes, and the short, feathered black hair that framed her valentine-shaped face. It was a haircut he disliked on most women, but somehow it worked on her. He drummed his fingers harder. She had some muscle and meat to her and she jiggled in all the right places beneath her uniform. He couldn't stop staring.

When she stood on tiptoe trying to get a look inside the front window, going for her billy club and not her sidearm, he knew he had to move. She was assertive but too optimistic.

He slid out of the 'Stang without closing the driver's door, moved silently in a wide arc so he'd come up directly behind her. She was still on tippy-toe and he liked the way the shadows edged her curves, the streetlamp casting a soft pale light and

the moon throwing off a much more vivid liquid silver, accenting every detail. Then someone inside
the shop knocked over a vase or some shit and the
noise made her stick the billy club back in her belt
and start to draw her .38. Goddamn idiots.

He sped up. She was sharp and fast enough to
sense him while he was still sneaking up on her.
He was maybe five feet away when she turned and
swung the barrel toward him. He dove at her, his
hand flashing out, and after a brief struggle in
which she tried to knee him, he managed to wrestle the gun free from her. She elbowed him in the
gut and came in again with a right cross to his
chin. It rattled his teeth and he saw stars, but once
he held her own pistol on her she settled back.
They faced each other.

She controlled her fear. Chase watched as she
tightened herself around it, tamping the panic
down, and he felt a surge of respect for her. It
wasn't easy to keep calm looking into a gun.

"You've got mean eyes," she said.

She should only run into Jonah. "If you think
so, then you've never really seen anybody with
mean eyes."

"I think I have."

"In this town? Get real."

It made him itchy, the way she looked at him,
and he hated holding on to the gun. He tossed it
from one hand to the other, like it was red-hot.

"My, but you're a fast one," she said.

"You've got some speed yourself, lady." It was about the finest compliment a driver could pay.

"You set that hotel fire?"

"It's just a smoker, I didn't want anyone hurt."

"People can still be hurt stampeding outta the building. You ever think'a that?"

He'd always hated the Southern accent until he heard it on her. There was flint in her voice, a lot of heat.

"Well, I am a bad guy," he said, reasonably. "Just not too bad."

"Stop doing that."

"Doing what?"

"Tossing that hardware. You're likely to shoot me without even meaning to."

Chase almost apologized. He relaxed his hold on the .38 and pointed it down at the sidewalk.

"There's somethin' truly goddamned infuriating about having your own gun aimed at you," she told him.

"I imagine there would be. But it's not really aimed at you."

"Too close to shave the difference." She lifted her chin and stuck her chest out. It was a pretty chin and a damn fine chest. "You gonna pull the trigger?"

"I thought we might avoid all that."

It made her firm up her bottom lip into a sexy but very serious pout. "You could've avoided it by refraining from scoring jewelry shops at near 1:00 A.M. in my hometown." She held her hand out. "You return that to me now and things will swing a lot easier for you, especially when I drag your ass before Judge Kelton in the morning."

"Let me ask you," Chase said, "what kind of antiques and rustic curios is Bookatee likely to have in this rustic curio emporium?"

She thought about it for a second, moonlight glazing her features. "I believe my cousin Ferdie once bought a stuffed gray squirrel dressed up like Robert E. Lee, with saber pointed skyward, astride his horse Traveler, from this here shop."

"Holy Christ, why?"

"I never asked."

A small tug in his chest grew stronger. He stared at her, really trying to reach deep and see what might be inside, what gave her such confidence and strength. But the mercury sheen cast against the side of her face faded as clouds passed by the moon, throwing a veil across her eyes.

"You're by far the cutest cop to ever draw down on me," he said.

"And you're just another damn outlaw, though younger than most I've seen."

Chase grinned. "And how many have you seen?"

"Including you and Cousin Ferdie, too damn many. But I reckon there might be time for you yet, to do the right thing. So why don't you try real hard to follow the smarter course?"

"You're not much older than me. How'd you become a deputy sheriff so young?"

"The sheriff is my daddy," she told him, "but don't let that fact fool you. I earned my way."

He nodded, sure that she had. "What's your name?"

That got the pout out again. "Why? You plan on sending me a postcard from Angola?"

He needn't have asked. What with the Southern hospitality and all that shit, she wore a name tag beneath her cop badge. Shadow-obscured but still readable.

Lila Bodeen.

The klutzes inside the store knocked over something else with a loud ka-klunk. She said, "Not too nimble, your friends."

"Not my friends either."

"Well then, what's a good ole boy like you want to boost a shop dedicated to improving the quality of life with curios anyway?"

"Trust me, I've been asking myself that repeatedly."

"You'd think a smart fella could have answered by now."

She wasn't going to give an inch, which made him like her even more. "Why aren't you at the hotel making sure all your traveling soap salesmen are getting out safely?"

"Somebody's got to keep an eye on the town. Just in case some less than savorish types might be using smoke to cover illegal actions of one sort or another."

A laugh rose from him as he turned her name

around and around in his head. He smiled and
tried to stamp a sweet expression onto his face.

She said, "I'm made of flesh and blood, not tinder. Those eyes aren't going to burn me down."

So much for the charm and wit being able to
work wonders. He could feel himself moving
toward her. She saw him about to take a step. She
misread his intentions and almost made a break
for it. He held his hands out palms up to show he
didn't mean anything, that he was harmless really,
but considering he still had his index finger in the
trigger guard of her .38, he figured he wasn't exactly getting the point across.

The crew came rushing out carrying a couple of
gunny sacks each. Hopefully the loot would be of
greater value than stuffed gray squirrels posed in
those The-South-Will-Rise-Again stances.

The three-man string stopped short and stared
at Deputy Sheriff Lila Bodeen. They didn't ask any
questions or run for the car or wait for Chase to
say anything. They started talking among themselves and quickly decided they wanted to kill her.

They threw down the sacks while they chat-
tered and Chase took a peek inside. He saw a lot of
crap and nothing that might be worth the fifteen
grand he'd expected from his share.

The string stood around arguing, discussing
Lila's murder like she wasn't there. Saying they
should give her a double tap to the back of the

head and dispose of her body in the hills near one of the old abandoned stills. The corpse might never be found. Another wanted to tie rocks to her feet and toss her in the river. They considered which rocks might work best and which method they should use to attach them to her feet. Ropes or chains, netting or mesh. They still had some TNT stashed, maybe they should blow her up. One of them wanted to rape her first. Then all of them did. Lila kept her face tight, doing her best to force out any fear.

Chase sighed and shot all three of the nitwits in the leg.

It made her jump, which was nice to see. She glanced at him and he was tinder, burning. He stuck the pistol in his belt and disarmed the others while they rolled around in the street yelping and gripping their wounds. Blood pulsed through their fingers. He told them to stop thrashing so much, it would just make them bleed faster. No one listened.

They didn't know his real name and even if they ever did run into anybody in prison that might recognize his description or skills, taking out these mooks would probably work in his favor.

He turned to Lila and said, "Okay, there you go. You just bagged a few more unsavorish types, cracked another gang of regional jewel thieves."

"Not all of them," she said. "There's still you."

"Start with these three. Your Judge Kelton will

give you a medal. Town this size, they might even throw you a parade."

"My daddy wouldn't let them. He believes in humility almost as much as he does justice. I want my pistol back."

"I hate guns. I'll leave it and the others on the curb when I pull out."

"You're not taking the boodle?"

Christ, maybe he really was in love. Boodle. Your heart had to skip at that. "I wouldn't be able to unload this shit anyway, they're the ones with the fence."

She cocked her head, studying him. He appreciated the way she looked at him, unsure but curious. She moistened her lips and the moon glistened in them. "You're the damn strangest outlaw I've ever run into."

He shrugged and backed away down the block. "Maybe we'll run into each other again."

"Stay in my town and you can count on it."

Well, all right then. "I might just do that."

He dropped the guns in the gutter, got in the 'Stang, and started to pull away from the curb. Before he could put the pedal down she was running for her cruiser, leaving the three geniuses still rolling in the road and clutching their legs. He thought it might be fun to get into a high-speed pursuit around here. He figured he could outdrive her easily, but she'd know these roads better. It would even it up, make things a little more interesting.

But no, that wasn't it, she was going for the shotgun in the trunk of the car. Jesus Christ. He watched her pull it free and cock it once as he went speeding by. It made him grin and he thought she was smiling too, a second before she blew out his back window.

That was the beginning.

Stealing different cars and following her around as best he could without being spotted, he watched her for two weeks. She was keen as hell and seemed to know he was out there keeping an eye on her. Always checking her rearview and making crazy U-turns, suspecting a tail and hoping to shake him out of the shadows.

There wasn't much to his mustache but he let it grow and eventually dyed it. It made him look like Fu Manchu planning to take down all of Western culture. He wore a baseball cap and a pair of sunglasses he picked up at Bookatee's Emporium.

The minute he stepped into the shithole store filled with Southern kitsch items—these people had a thing about stuffed animals, a shellacked bullfrog, the hell was up with this part of the country?—he was filled with a new sense of pride for having shot the crew for choosing this place to knock over.

There were maybe fifty Jeb Stuart statues and Dixie flags hanging from the rafters. Guns, Bowie knives, plenty of Civil War pistols and cutlasses in the cases. The antique jewelry was right back on display. Some of it looked fairly impressive. He paid three bucks for the sunglasses, put them on, and thought for maybe the hundredth time, What am I doing?

Tuesday was her day off. She went out to a matinee with a chunky friend of hers, poofy frizzy hair out to here, bad skin, the two of them heading down to the Piper Cub Movie Theater. It doubled as a place where country bands played on weekends, folks hopping out of their seats, yee-hawing and dancing in the aisles.

No chick flicks for Lila, she liked the bang-'em-ups. This one was about terrorists who take a cutie-pie ten-year-old girl hostage and she turns out to be some secret government assassin trained since birth. Pretty soon she's flying a jet at Mach 2.0 and handling a high-powered rifle with laser sighting, icing evil dictators. Chase had seen the trailer on his rented room's television and thought it looked like it might be a decent way to kill a couple of hours.

He was staying at a boardinghouse two counties west, almost forty miles away, stealing cars over there just in case Lila's father was still scouting around for his Mustang. The lady who ran the house was crocked on lightning half the time and never quit listening to Conway Twitty. There was a framed picture of the guy hanging on the wall over Chase's bed where you usually found Jesus or Elvis. Chase felt a little uncomfortable with Conway looking down over him like that, especially considering the weirdo hair on that fucker.

A pretty big crowd at the theater for a Tuesday morning, lots of toughs with torn-off sleeves who carried snap knives on their belts. A group of teenage girls clamoring for attention, blouses tied at the midriff, showing off their belly-button rings. He wondered if they went in for Conway too.

Everybody knew Lila and they cooled their action when she walked by. Her friend was loud and talked a lot on her cell phone while they paid for their tickets.

Playing with the mustache, the damn thing driving him crazy, Chase hung in close enough to hear the friend's name—Molly Mae—and tried to think of a way to get her out of there. She was an attention hound, practically shouting into her phone at somebody named Hoyt, telling him to fix the busted axle on Lottie Belle's—seriously, you can't mean it, Lottie Belle?—truck or she wasn't going to make briarberry pie this Saturday. Chase tried to figure out how to use this information to his advantage but came up empty.

He needn't have bothered. Turned out she was going to help him. At the candy counter she picked up a Mega-Box of popcorn, three candy bars, and a Jumbo Coke, the thing going forty ounces. She'd have to break for the bathroom by the end of the second reel.

The little-girl assassin was poking out the eyes of a big bearded guy in a turban when Molly Mae made a beeline up the aisle and disappeared through the door into the lobby.

Chase's pulse twisted in his neck, and with death on the screen and maybe a jail term coming up due to this next move, his mind wandered back to a scene of happiness when he was a kid. His mother and father dancing in the living room on New Year's, their laughter forever alive inside him. Their deaths forever seared into him. A thief never followed his heart, he always planned every move out and had at least three escape routes in place. You scored or you ran. Chase fought the instincts ingrained in him by his grandfather. He understood with a sudden clarity that he was terri-fied of his own mounting loneliness, for fear he would become even more like Jonah.

Chase slid next to Lila, easing into Molly Mae's seat, and put his feet up on the chair in front of him. She'd left some of her candy behind and in the darkness he plucked a few pieces out of the box.

The little killer chick was crying about her lack of a normal childhood and the government black ops and scientists who'd created her were making speeches about fighting for the American Way. A few moments later she was chopping the main villain in the throat as a nuclear bomb ticked down. Chase kept trying to think of something slick to say and thought maybe he had it now. He opened his mouth.

Without turning to look at him, Deputy Sheriff Lila Bodeen pressed a snub .32 into his ribs and said, "Now that there is one hell of a disguise, stranger."

Okay, now he needed something else to say instead. Nothing was coming, the bomb beeping at ninety-nine, ninety-eight, ninety-seven—

"But what do you think of the mustache?" he asked.

"Is it real or is that a rat's ass glued to your lip?"

Christ, that was a much better line than anything he could come up with. She was going to trounce him at this. "Only one way to discover the truth. You'll have to gather the empirical datum on your own."

She frowned, the bright light from the screen igniting the furrows in her brow. "You one of them college-educated outlaws?"

Someone shushed them and they leaned their heads closer together.

"No," he whispered. "The fat scientist guy just told the little vicious chick that."

Lila nodded and dug the .32 in deeper, and Chase ground his back teeth together. She said, "Do I take it you've been struck with a case of conscience and are planning on turning yourself in?"

"I just wanted to watch the movie."

"I admit I was liking it myself. Now the call of justice will interrupt me on my day off."

"I regret that," Chase said. He let out a chuckle, feeling cool but not cold. A nervous tremor worked through him for a lot of reasons besides the fact that an extra foot-pound of pressure from her index finger would blast his spleen over the teenage couple sitting behind him.

"Be a shame if you had to waste your $3.25 matinee money," he said. "How about if you turn me in afterward?"

"You think I won't?" Lila asked.

"Let's find out."

It was then that Molly Mae returned from the ladies' room and said, "Who's this roughneck that's been eatin' my peanut clusters!"

After gathering up her remaining candy, Molly Mae picked up on the undercurrents, maybe spotted the gleam of the gun in Chase's ribs, and with a huff that blew more poof into her poofy hair, she moved an aisle down.

The assassin girl defused the bomb, discovered the whereabouts of her real parents, tried to act like a normal girl but eventually garotted a terrorist in front of her mother's coffee klatch, and finally decided to go live with the scientists again. Chase and Lila finished watching the film and sat in their seats, nodding as her friends and neighbors walked by, his bruised ribs really starting to kill him, until the theater completely emptied.

She said, "Guess it's time to escort you over to the jail."

"Nice day out. Maybe we can walk it."

"You're taking this lightly."

"No, I'm not. It'll give me a chance to breathe in my last bit of fresh air for a while."

"I suppose we can do that. Especially since Molly Mae drove and you done run her off with your peanut cluster heist."

Lila tried hard to keep from smiling but couldn't entirely manage it. She grinned, her chin dimpling, her eyes on him but not looking into his. A rush of warmth brimmed inside him and he thought, Maybe this is how you beat the cold spot, this is how you stay out of that place.

He said, "It was about as worthy a score as knocking over Bookatee's Emporium was."

"Don't you tell her that though."

So they walked through town toward the police station, and he found himself rambling about how the last three years had gone, saying nothing of Jonah, nothing of his mother's murder or his old man's suicide. People waved to Lila and she waved back with her free hand, the snub jutting into his side every once in a while, mostly hidden by her purse. Chase smiled and waved too.

"Judge Kelton didn't show much mercy on your friends."

"I told you, they weren't my friends."

"Your former crew?"

"Hardly. When thieves working together aren't all that tight we call it a string. Those idiots weren't even that."

"You probably shouldn't have gotten involved with them then, a stand-up professional villain like yourself."

"I know it. I needed some quick money."

"It's only an assumption on my part," Lila said, the "my" coming out mostly as "ma," "but I'm guessing that's what every thief says just about every time he's doing any thieving."

It wasn't true, but he liked listening to her.

When they got to the police station she marched him up the front steps to the door. A couple of deputies moved in and out. Chase really hoped he hadn't misread the whole situation, because if he had, he was going to have to cut and run now, and probably take a bullet in the spine.

He turned and faced her, pressing her back against the brick building. Now the snub was in his belly. He almost went in for a kiss, but veered off at the last second. She'd flattened her lips, still trying to read him and figure out what she was dealing with. It was good to know he wasn't the only one who was confused.

"This is a helluva dangerous way to woo a girl," Lila said.

"Yeah, but is it effective?"

"I've had worse dates," she told him.

"Yeah?"

"You don't want to hear about them and I don't want to relive 'em."

"No, I suppose not. Well, here we are at the halls of justice."

"Yeah," she said, showing just a flash of teeth. "Time for your just reward."

The gun in his guts didn't hurt that much, but the smile—like a knife in the heart.

*A few days later, while they lay in bed in a rough-*and-tumble spot called the Skeeter Motel—these people just didn't think their names through down here—Lila asked him about his parents, how he'd wound up such a young outlaw. He was starting to like it when she called him that.

Chase had already told her a lot about Jonah, but this was different. He did what he'd trained himself to do, separating himself from his emotions and keeping memories of his childhood as blunt as possible, letting the words drop from him like stones.

He lit a cigarette and took a couple of deep drags. His voice took on the hollow ring he expected, and he smoked and listened to the person speaking as if it was somebody familiar whom he hadn't heard from in a long time. The man spoke fast.

"Nine years ago my mother was murdered, shot through the head in our kitchen. She was eight months pregnant."

"Sweet Jesus—did you . . . ?"

"No, I didn't see it. I was at school. So was my father. He was a college professor who taught world literature. After her funeral, we'd visit her grave every day. He was wrecked. It was a bad winter, but we'd go out there and stand in the snow, sometimes for hours. Even back then I knew it was at least a little crazy."

"He was grief-struck," Lila said.

"There are only so many prayers you can say. He was out of his head and stayed there. He'd recite poetry and scenes from Greek plays. He was soft."

"He was doing the best he could."

"Sometimes that's enough and sometimes it's not," Chase said. "He'd get drunk on whiskey. So would I. It was all we had to keep us warm out there in the cemetery. He used to sink to his knees and hold on to me while he wept. Sometimes he'd pass out from exhaustion or just because he was bombed. I'd stand there with ice in my hair, loaded on scotch, and try to keep him from freezing to death."

Not exactly the best postcoital topic of conversation, but he knew Lila was the one, and he was glad she'd asked. He had his arm around her and raised his hand to brush the hair from her face.

She reached for his cigarette and took a few

puffs, handed it back to him. "And you're angry with your father for that?"

"I guess I sound like it, don't I?"

"Because he acted weak in front of you. Because you were so young, and he put all of that responsibility on your shoulders. So you hated him."

"Not about that so much as what came next," Chase admitted. "After the cops hit a brick wall with their investigation, my father asked a newscaster if he could go on television and appeal to the killer. The newscaster said he thought that instead of my dad doing the pleading, I should do it instead. Maybe I'd warm the murderer's heart. Like he'd suddenly crack and give himself up."

A tiny groan drifted from the back of Lila's throat. "And I said that thing to you about your being struck with a case of conscience and turning yourself in." She gently pressed her lips to his neck. "I'm sorry for that."

"When you said it, it was funny."

"I'm not so sure about that."

"But what they wanted me to do, it was stupid, just a ratings ploy. But I was a kid and had no say. They put cameras and lights on me and instructed me on what to do. When my eyes didn't look wet enough they made me repeat my performance. When they still weren't wet enough, they used glycerin on my cheeks. There was a makeup woman and somebody kept coming over and brushing my hair. It was like a movie set. Me doing twelve takes begging the man who killed my mother to give it up. Looking left, then right, then straight on while they decided which was my best side."

"I like 'em both."

"Yeah?"

"Yep. Now that the mustache is gone, anyways."

"They put mascara on me to thicken my eyelashes."

"It was callous and cruel," Lila said, "that's for sure, but still, it's understandable. If they had no hard evidence or suspects after the first few days, the police would've been willing to try damn near anything. They wanted to get the killer."

"That's the logical, adult way of thinking about it. But my head is still wrapped up in what I saw and felt back then. That afternoon, my old man, he looked like he'd swallowed rat poison. Later, my father and I watched the news together. He sat around waiting, like the killer might phone him up and apologize. My dad was already mostly out of his head but now he went even further. I knew he was going to kill himself, and there was nothing I could do about it."

"You were just a little boy."

Chase shrugged, ground the cigarette out against the side of the nightstand.

Lila sat up, propped by the pillows and took his face in her hands. It felt like the most natural kind of touch in the world, and he knew he'd never felt it before. "You were already proving yourself tough and strong, bearing up under that kind of pain."

"Maybe that's why Jonah came back for me. Just because I made it through. Even my father buckled and went out the easy way."

She stiffened and frowned. "I'm not sure that's such a generous comment to make about your own daddy."

"It's not, but it's hard to feel charitable to someone who quits the game and leaves you on your own at ten years old."

"I'm guessing if he could've found another way, he would've. Not everyone is made of the sternest stuff."

"No."

"So what happened to him?"

There was the question. He saw his father again, holding a bottle of whiskey to his chest as if it might somehow save him. The snow mounting on the tombstones, the man as cold outside of her grave as she was in it.

"He had a sailboat. We used to go out on the Great South Bay during the summers. One morning, about a month after the murder, we were expecting another blizzard. I got ready to go to the cemetery as always, but instead he drove down to the marina. He started to dig his boat out of the ice with an ax. The bay itself wasn't frozen, just the edges of the channel where the boats were docked. People drove by and called to him but he ignored everyone. He didn't say a word to me. I said nothing either. When he got too tired, he looked at me like he might begin crying again, so I took over chopping the ice. Eventually the boat got loose. He left me on the dock. Climbed on board and took it out of the bay and toward the ocean channels. I lost sight of him fast. The storm hit maybe an hour later. I hitchhiked back to the house."

Lila's lips drew together, bloodless.

Chase said, "You're not liking him so much anymore, are you."

"I just wish he'd found another way. One where you weren't dragged in so deep."

"The wreckage washed up on Fire Island that night. His body was never found. Probably threw himself overboard as soon as he was far enough from shore that the tide wouldn't take him back in. Has a romantic kind of quality to it, I think. Going out like Shelley and Hart Crane."

"I don't know who they are."

"It doesn't matter."

"He didn't say anything at all to you before he sailed off?" she asked, her fingers tangled in his chest hair.

Chase thought, I shouldn't be talking about this. I should've kept it under control. We ought to be laughing, rolling over each other, getting ready for another bout. I'm doing her a disservice.

"No," Chase told her.

"Didn't have the heart to kill himself right in front of you, so he just slipped away." She looked into his eyes, figuring him out a little more now. "He thought he was doing a kindness to you, but that was the worst part, wasn't it."

"I don't know."

"You know it really wasn't his fault. There's no shame in having a nervous breakdown 'cause of such misery. He loved your mama so much, some people can't go on brokenhearted like that."

Saying nothing because there was nothing to say, Chase drew Lila to him and kissed her. The solidity of her body on his connected him not only to the world but somehow also to himself. What had been kept frozen in the cold spot for so long was beginning to warm and loosen. He had always thought of his father as fragile, perhaps even cowardly, but now he saw the man in a different way. A new perspective, thanks to Lila.

"So how'd you wind up with Jonah?" she asked.

"My old man wasn't considered legally dead yet so the house and bank accounts were all tied up in court. I had no relatives I knew of and was sent to live with a foster family. A rich, sweet, older couple, the kind of folks whose favorite game is reading random quotes from the Bible and seeing who can guess the chapter and verse. They had a couple kids of their own and had taken in another six or seven to care for. All different colors and nationalities. Half with prosthetics of some kind. One girl with her face badly disfigured with burns. All of us in a huge home on the North Shore of Long Island."

"And you were eyeing the silverware."

Even now, she got him grinning. "I wasn't with the family long. After only about a month Jonah showed up at the front door one day and said, 'I'm your father's father. You never heard of me, have you?' I hadn't and told him so. He said, 'We're blood, that's important, and you've got a choice. You can stay with these people and live life on the map, or you can come along with me.'"

"Life on the map?"

"I didn't even know what it meant, but he said it in such a way that I understood and believed him. He said, 'It won't be pretty, some of it, but it's a part of who you are.' So I went with him."

"Just like that?"

"Yeah. My foster parents raised hell while I was packing, but they were scared of Jonah. He sat in a chair in the living room and stared at them until I was done. The girl with the burned face wanted to come too, if you can believe it."

"She liked you, and the two best sides of your face."

"No, she liked Jonah. His strength and his calm. So I just walked off the map and out of the system. I didn't want school and a college education. My mother died in her quaint kitchen. My father was a professor. I wanted to be anyone but them."

"An outlaw from the start."

"I guess so."

With a slight shrug against the sheets, Lila

curled beside him, and the dried sweat on her flesh *scritched* against his own. "What would your daddy think of the way your life's been going these last few years?"

Chase thought about it, looking up, scanning the ceiling as if searching for the man. He lit another cigarette and smoked it all down to the filter. Lila was still staring at him, expecting an answer. He tried to give her one.

"I don't really care. He made his choice and I made mine."

The next day, Lila invited him back to her place. A single-story house off in the woods, pretty much on its own, maybe two miles down the road from her parents', three or four from the center of town where the police station was. He'd followed her here a couple times and cased the place. He showed her what was wrong with the locks on her windows and how easy it was to break in the back door.

"How romantic," she told him, "sharing methods on home invasion prevention."

He shrugged. "I stick to my strengths."

She made roasted wild turkey and stuffing with sharp, tangy flavors he'd never tasted before. While they sat there eating, without the need always to fill the silence, he realized with some surprise that this was his very first date.

He'd lost his virginity at thirteen when Jonah

had brought home two waitresses from a truck stop in Cedar Rapids, where they'd been working a short grift picking up a few easy bucks. Jonah had brought other women around before but no relationship had ever lasted more than a couple of weeks.

Carrying a mostly empty pint of Dewar's, Jonah introduced both ladies as Lou, which got them giggling. He said their names again and they guffawed so hard they had to sit down. Chase didn't get the joke, but what the hell.

The whiskey reek coming off them filled the room like smoke from a three-alarm fire. Chase couldn't handle the smell anymore, not since the days when his father had taken bottles to the cemetery. His stomach tumbled and he began to breathe shallowly.

The cute Lou turned out to be Louise, who gave Chase the eye and licked her lips. She got up and lurched toward him, saying she wanted to dance. She hummed in his ear and pressed her huge breasts to him, where they wobbled proudly. She whispered how she liked younger men because they could ride in the saddle all night long. He'd never heard it called that before, but he was a bright kid and could pick up on the metaphor. It tightened his guts and scared the shit out of him, but the heat rising through his body seared away any doubts.

The much less cute Lou was Lulu, who was nearly unconscious but still making the effort to hang in there. She gave Chase an unfocused gaze where her eyes mostly crossed. Her chin fell to her chest as she struggled to stay awake. Her teeth were smeared with red lipstick.

Chase looked at Jonah and realized his grandfather, who never drank on a job, was stone sober.

It was only when cute Lou was about to dance off to the bedroom with Chase that Jonah put his arm around her in a blatant territorial gesture. No subtlety there, no mistaking the meaning. He held up a hand to Chase's chest, not quite touching him, grasping the girl tightly under his wing.

So there it was. Chase got the chick who was nearly out cold for his first lay. Before he could do anything he made her brush her teeth and gargle. It still didn't kill the whiskey smell, and for the eight minutes he was in the saddle he had to keep his face turned away from hers.

It was terrible, but at least he didn't have to take the blame for the general lack of success all by himself. In the morning, it didn't seem to matter. Lulu didn't remember much. They went for a second bout on the couch that was much better than the first go-around.

At Lila's dinner table, thinking of Lulu made him realize all the more what he'd been missing for so long.

After they'd finished eating she said, "Let's have wine in the den."

He looked around the place. "You don't have a den."

"Sure I do, there's even a fireplace."

"Most folks call that the bedroom," he told her.

Holding up the bottle of wine, easing him along as she pressed forward, she said,"That right?"

Afterward, while he was catching his breath, she asked him again about his past.

It was getting a little spooky now, always talking about the worst things that had ever happened to him while her chest was powdered with salt and his neck burned with her teeth marks.

He slid aside and stared into the cold fireplace, wondering why anybody in Mississippi would ever need one in their house, much less in the bedroom. It was October and nearly eighty degrees outside.

"I always wondered what it would've been like," he said, "if my old man had been able to hold on. If he could've ever bounced back from being so broken. But Jonah told me I would be better off without my father. Maybe he was right."

Lila tensed and reared up, giving him the pout, and brought her small, hard fist down on his belly. It hurt and he gasped.

"Don't you say that."

"Ouch."

"Don't you ever say such a thing, you hear me now?"

"All right."

"Fathers are important."

She was so powerful in her presence, standing up for people she'd never meet, who were already nearly ten years dead. He'd never shared so much with anyone before.

As the sun went down, the shadows lanced the bedroom, growing thicker second by second, stabbing across the sheets. The window was open, a breeze stirring the lace curtains. Despite having shoved his childhood behind locked doors, he could still hear an occasional noise come through. Now he heard the sound of his old man chopping at the ice with an ax, needing to die so badly.

"I hope he's not dead," Chase said.

"Your daddy?"

He let out a small snort of surprise. "No, the man who murdered my mother and the baby. I can't let go of the idea that one of these days I might get a chance to kill him."

PART

II

Lila introduced her father as Sheriff Bodeen. A woman introduces her father as something other than Dad or Daddy and you know you've got a situation on your hands.

Sheriff Bodeen hated Chase's guts from the first minute. Bodeen smiled like a three-day-old corpse and kept chuckling under his breath, trying to be a good ole boy. Going, Heh heh heh. Eh heh heh. The sound lifted the hair on Chase's neck.

Bodeen stood about five-foot-two and had short-guy syndrome, needed to prove he was the toughest son of a bitch in any room he walked into. He had arms thick as tree trunks and with every step he sort of exploded across the room. All riptide energy.

His brown uniform was immaculately clean and pressed, buttoned to the throat. He kept his gun belt on. The strap over the butt of his .45 had been

snapped loose. This for Sunday dinner, meeting
his daughter's boyfriend for the first time.

When Bodeen hugged Lila he made a spectacle
out of it, like he hadn't seen her for years. Swept
her up, twirled her around, kept calling her his little girl, his buttercup. She went with it. Finally he
put her down and she left the room to check on
the chicken-fried steak she was making for dinner.

Her mother was the quietest woman Chase had
ever met. Really big, burly actually, with a lot of
muscle to her. She hugged him hello. He couldn't
get his arms all the way around her, it was like
grabbing hold of the front end of a Toyota. She
squeezed him until he thought his ribs were about
to go.

These people, he thought, Christ, there's a lot
of undercurrent here, forget that Southern hospitality shit.

Lila flashed in and out of the living room, either giving him time to get used to her parents or
really busy cooking. He had stared at the stuff
stewing and boiling in the pots and pans and had
no idea what side dishes they'd be eating tonight.

She'd told him to call her mother Mama, but
Chase couldn't do it. He went with her first name.
Hester.

Keeping up the friendly front, Bodeen called
Chase "son" a lot, but there was serious ice in his
eyes, a lot of rage and resentment. It would come
out eventually, Chase knew, he just had to wait
for it.

The man asked a lot of questions about Chase's background. Started off casually but got more and more personal while they sat and waited. He drank a lot of whiskey with a lot of ice and appeared a little put off that Chase was sticking to beer.

Chase knew his name had already been run through the system by Bodeen, and the man would be wondering about all the gaps and holes. Lila had come up with a pretty complicated and convincing backstory that would hopefully divert any doubts. It was so involved and complex that Chase couldn't remember any of it.

Bodeen would know about Chase's mother being murdered. Jonah had been off the map for too long; Chase didn't think anybody would ever find a connection between the two of them, but you just couldn't tell. There might be some small scrap of computer info. Or somebody in the bent life might've flipped and given up everything he knew about everybody he knew. It was a chance Chase would take for Lila. They could always run if it came down to that.

Her parents had him pinned in the living room. Hester sat to the left of Chase, sipping a tumbler of rye and patting and rubbing his wrist. It was a vaguely sensual display and really threw him off.

Bodeen, squashing him on the right, said, "You plan on staying in these parts?"

"Yes," Chase said.

"Never knew anyone from the North who could last more than a year down this way."

"I've been in the South for almost four."

"On the move."

"That's right."

"Why's that?" Bodeen asked.

"Because I've been alone."

"And now you're not so you think you wanna settle down. But I'm talking about roots. It's a different way of life. We still speak like somebody. We have the advantage of not being as homogenized as other places."

Bodeen's use of "homogenized" impressed Chase. It was a word his father had used. He could just imagine his old man sitting here, trying hard to fit in and get along, making the effort not to discuss Russian literature. Maybe saying, "Boy, it's humid!" because when you got down to it, there wasn't a hell of a lot of middle ground where they could meet.

"I think I'm taking to it just fine so far."

"Because of Lila."

"Yes, because of her."

Hester smiled at him and kept touching his wrist. Chase smiled back. She smiled more. He tried to smile more but just couldn't do it, it was tiring his face out. Bodeen finished another glass of whiskey and started chewing the ice.

Lila poked her head out of the kitchen and said, "Dinner's almost ready."

Bodeen told her, "Me and the boy are gonna

have a quick smoke out back," and Chase thought, Here it comes, here it is.

"You smoke after dinner, Daddy, not before."

"I smoke whenever the hell I want and that's just so. We'll be back in a couple a minutes."

Chase walked out the back door with the man and accepted the unfiltered Camel offered from a soft pack. He used to smoke on occasion with the crews but hadn't had a cigarette since that poker game, when he'd split the filters and flushed them down the toilet hoping the others wouldn't cap him like they'd done Walcroft.

The smoke burned in his mouth. Bodeen leaned in as if to say something but didn't. Just rocked back on his heels, then bent forward again. He did it three or four times before getting in close and whispering, "I'll give you twenty-four hours."

Chase asked, "For what?"

"To get out of town."

At least it was right there out in the open now. "That so?"

"I don't want you 'round my little girl."

"Why's that?"

"She deserves better."

"You're probably right. But for argument's sake, who would you consider better?"

"Anybody but you."

"Now you're just being mean."

"Maybe yes, maybe no, but it's a daddy's right." Bodeen took a long drag, let it out slow. Turned that gaze on Chase again, really sizzling it in. "I can smell the bad on you. You gonna try and deny that?"

"No."

"So, by this time tomorrow, you be gone."

"No."

"What's that now?"

"I love her and I'm not leaving."

Chase thought if Bodeen pulled his gun now this whole situation was going to step up a notch, so he might as well do it himself. His hand flashed out and he snatched the .45 from its holster and tossed it over his shoulder into the mud.

Get the ball rolling, let's see where this leads us.

Sheriff Bodeen stared at him and let the smile ease out again, inch by inch. "You're a fast one," he said.

Same thing his daughter had first said to Chase.

Chase thought if it was going to work with Lila he would have to do something to impress her father. That meant a slug-out or some kind of insanity like duck hunting. He stepped forward in case the sheriff wanted to take a poke at him. So long as it wasn't in the kidneys, it would be worth it.

"Yeah," Chase said, and finished a last drag on the cigarette and flicked the butt in the dirt.

A knowing, crooked smile split Sheriff Bodeen's face. Like a lot of cops, he enjoyed finding a player. Someone in the know he could legally beat the shit out of.

Bodeen nodded, said, "Let me tell you something, son. You don't ever throw a man's pistol in the dirt. It's disrespectful. It's uncivilized."

Then with a mulish bellow, he lunged.

Chase thinking, Frickin' terrific.

The sheriff caught him in the left ribs with a hell of a shot. The air burst from Chase's lungs and he went over backward and hit the ground hard. Black streamers appeared at the edges of his vision, but as he gasped for breath he still had sense enough to roll aside as fast as he could.

He tucked in tight because Bodeen was coming at him again. Chase got to his knees and took a kick in the gut and a quick one-two punch to the head that sent him spinning in the grass. But at least he'd bought a little time, and now he was breathing again.

Cracking his knuckles, Bodeen postured for a moment. Good, the guy was flawed. He imagined eyes on him. He wanted to show off for the crowd. Chase managed to get to his feet, trying to remember the boxing lessons Jonah had given him years ago.

He got his fists up and deflected a couple of Bodeen's jabs. The man was strong but not very quick, and Chase had an extra few inches of reach over the short fucker. The man came on with another flurry and tagged both Chase's eyes, which immediately started to water.

Bodeen started to chuckle, enjoying himself. And why not, Chase hadn't landed a punch yet. He had a hell of a time focusing, his mind stuffed with clutter and loud with too many voices. Jonah telling him to pick up the gun and shoot the cop. Jonah telling him to get on his toes, dance forward, work the bridge of the nose. His father explaining that violence was a sign of character weakness. His mother crying—why was she crying? She seemed to be crying so much there at the end. Why? He hadn't thought about that since he was a kid.

Lowering his arms an inch, Chase baited Bodeen into throwing a wild roundhouse. He dodged and gunned four rapid-fire shots into the sheriff's belly, hearing the man's grunts grow louder and more pained each time he connected. It felt good. He danced away, kicking up tufts of grass, then came in again and worked Bodeen's nose.

Snapping his knuckles hard across the bridge, over and over, wanting to leave his mark. Blood burst from Bodeen's nostrils and the man let out another little laugh. Everything funny to this guy. The Jonah inside Chase's head said, Look out.

Chase tried to move back a step, but Bodeen charged again, those squat muscular legs really letting him explode. The force carried him through Chase's defenses. One of those huge fists landed directly over Chase's heart. His blood flow felt like it reversed course for a second and he stood paralyzed. Even his knees wouldn't fold to let him drop out of range. Bodeen took his time to line up his next shot and brought a right crashing into

Chase's chin. It was a hell of a nice move. Chase felt the hinges of his jaw break and wondered how much it was going to cost to get it wired.

Maybe duck hunting would've been the way to go.

He fell back and hit the dirt, gagging from the incredible pain and spitting blood. He'd botched this whole play. He should've been listening more closely to Jonah.

He wanted one more chance to prove himself to the sheriff. He struggled to turn over, got on all fours, and carefully made it to his feet. Bodeen laughed some more, going, Heh heh heh. Eh heh heh. What the fuck was that all about anyway? Chase let it slide. The sheriff's hands had lowered, but when he got a look at Chase's eyes he brought them back up again.

Jonah said, You idiot, cheat already.

Staggering, Chase found the cold spot. The pain faded away beneath the freeze, but his head was still loud with noise and need.

"You sure can handle pain, boy," Bodeen said. "We're done here."

Chase tried to say, Not yet, but when he opened his mouth all that came out was a huge wad of blood. He tried to grin but his jaw slid out of alignment and it felt like his tongue had flopped loose over his bottom lip.

Chase asked Jonah, So what now?

Jonah told him, He favors his left leg. Kick the kneecap out.

Sound advice, and not much of a cheat under the circumstances. So Chase brought an elbow down hard against Bodeen's hip, shifted his weight, and lashed out with his left foot. He connected with the sheriff's kneecap and felt the tendons go. Bodeen's leg broke with a small pop and he let out a shriek that spooked an oak tree full of egrets into flight.

Now get the .45 and kill him, Jonah said.

Bodeen toppled backward and writhed in the scrub grass, moaning but still letting loose a chuckle here and there. Weird son of a bitch.

Starting forward, Chase wobbled and dropped onto his ass, turned over onto his side and stretched out, trying to get air. They lay in the yard almost on top of each other, gasping loudly.

"You gonna make...my daughter a proper woman?" the sheriff asked.

Chase didn't know what the hell Bodeen was talking about now. He had to hold both palms tightly to the sides of his jaw in order to make it work well enough for him to speak. The pain was electric and unbelievable. "Lila is a...proper...woman." Strings of blood looped from his lips.

"A proper wife."

"Oh. Yeah...I am."

Bodeen was trying to put his kneecap back into place but as he gingerly touched his leg he let out another howl that ended in laughter. The sheriff lumbered up on his good leg and dragged the other behind him, limping around in circles until he found his gun. He stood and offered a hand. "Come on, son, let's go eat some greens."

But Chase wasn't going to eat anything solid for a while. Lila's mother pretended not to notice the blood and bruises when they dragged their asses back inside, which made sitting down to dinner even more fucking creepy. He figured he'd already earned whatever points he needed to earn. Hester just kept smiling. He was starting to think maybe this lady here had some serious emotional problems.

Lila brought him an ice pack and shot a death glare at her father, but she said nothing to the man. She got Chase on his feet and told him, "Come on along, we gotta get you to a hospital." He tried to wink at her but his eyes were closing up.

Hester smiled some more. This solid, hefty lady saying nothing, it felt like she was another aspect of his own lost mother. He was doomed to be surrounded by a mother's silent ghost.

They got to the door and Bodeen, clutching at his twisted leg in his chair, said, "What about me? You ain't worried your daddy might be crippled for life?" Trying to play it off as tough but with a touch of whine in his voice.

Lila left Chase propped in the doorway, walked back to her father, geared up, and with the side of her hand chopped him in the throat.

Sheriff Bodeen squawked like a strangled cat and

flopped against the dining-room table. Lila told him, "Daddy, you ever touch my man again and I'll make sure you ride all the way to hell in a wheelchair."

Hearing her say "my man" like that made Chase grin, and as she pulled his arm around her shoulder again, his tongue spilled out one side of his mouth and a thick rope of blood trailed from the other.

The next Saturday Sheriff Bodeen showed up at Lila's door on crutches with his leg in a cast. Chase backed up a step when he saw the man on the porch. He was still pissing blood and had already lost five pounds from having to eat meals through a straw. The fight had given him a certain sense about himself, knowing he could be hard when he had to be and that he could disregard Jonah when necessary. But still, he didn't feel like going another round right now.

The sheriff said, "You want a job?"

It was tough to talk but he could swing it. "What job?"

"I need another deputy. I could use someone like you."

"What's that mean?"

"What's what mean, son?"

"Someone like me."

"You're smart, you're fast, you're tough as saddle leather, and you know how to keep your head in the middle of a fight."

He thought about that for a minute. What a gas Jonah would have, thinking about Chase walking around with a badge. Standing there on a street corner being Deputy Dawg while Lila called him an outlaw. Riding after the stupid Southern crews that stumbled into town loaded on moonshine.

Chase said, "Thanks anyway."

Bodeen nodded, looked a little irritated, said, "You mind tellin' me why the hell not?"

"I don't like guns."

A couple of months later, when he started looking around for a wedding ring, he asked folks who the best jeweler in the area was. They all pushed him to Bookatee. He couldn't believe it, and nearly hit the road to go check out shops in New Orleans, St. Louis, Oklahoma City, somewhere there was civilization. But he figured what the hell and went to visit the Emporium.

Turned out Bookatee really did know jewelry. Book sold Chase a nice diamond ring for a fair price. When Book opened his safe and Chase got a look inside, he pursed his lips, realizing the crew really had known what they were doing. At least in scoring Bookatee.

*   *   *

He sent a message to Jonah only once, through the regular channels. From a pay phone he called Murphy in Fort Wayne, Indiana.

"Heard you were down South someplace," Murphy said.

"Still am."

"You looking for a job? I know of two shops that could use a good mechanic like you."

The usual way of telling him there were two crews looking for a wheelman. "No thanks. I think I'm settling down here for a while."

"Doing what? Changing oil? Rotating tires? Fixing crankshafts?"

Asking him what grifts he was working. "My crankshaft is just fine. I met a girl."

Chase could sense Murphy wrinkling his brow, trying to figure out what Chase was talking about, what kind of score he was after.

Chase said, "A real girl, Murph. I'm settling down."

"Kid like you who's been in the life since you were a squirt, it's got to be hard."

"Well, I'm getting married anyway."

"To one of them Southern belles? She the kind who expects you to sit in the stands of the Alabama-Mississippi game and cheer for the Muskrats or the Armadillos or whatever the fuck their mascots are?"

"No, she's the local sheriff's daughter."

"You do like a life of juice. What if big daddy decides to pull you in?"

"She already tried it. She's the deputy. He only broke my jaw."

Murphy let loose with a wild laugh. "Like most of you speedsters, you like to put the hammer down as far as it'll go."

"Only when I have to. I need to get a message to Jonah. I'd like to send him an invitation to the wedding."

"You're kidding."

"No."

"He'll steal the icing off the cake. Hold on." Murphy rolled around his office in a chair with squeaky casters, opening and closing filing cabinets. "He opened his own shop." Murphy rattled off ten digits. It wasn't exactly a sophisticated code. Chase reversed the number and saw it was a 202 prefix. Jonah was in DC.

He wasn't sure how it would go, talking to his grandfather again after all this time. He figured it would be easier for Jonah to get in touch with him if the man felt like it. Chase gave Murphy the reverse of his cell phone. "Tell him what I said. If he wants to, he can drop me a line."

The wedding got a little wonky because Lila had three moonshine-toting uncles who came out of the deep woods for the first time in years and started kicking it up hard. Chase liked them fine, but Sheriff Bodeen sat there eating fried possum and glowering as if he wanted to arrest them. And this was his best man, the father of the bride.

First came the drinking, then a lot of the food and some dancing, and then the actual service down at the lake. Everybody set up chairs with parasols affixed to them to keep the sun off their heads. They wreathed themselves in veils of mosquito netting. A choir of gospel singers led them all through a couple of quiet hymns before really getting funky, dancing around with their tambourines and howling out praises to Jesus.

Chase and Lila exchanged vows in front of a minister who was overcome with the Holy Ghost and started speaking in tongues. He threw himself into the lake and Chase had to dive in and fish him out. They both stood there dripping while the man finished the ceremony, Lila unable to look at Chase for fear of cracking up.

When he and Lila kissed everybody let out a Rebel yell.

She drew back and said, "Well, you're in it now, outlaw."

"Been that way since the moment you botched the grand curio shop heist."

A few of her friends wondered where his family was and asked a lot of personal questions. He gave the usual short-shrift answers, smiling but definitely putting some ice into his words, and eventually they backed off. The three drunk toothless uncles started firing shotguns in the air and actually managed to nail a couple of wild geese. They plucked the birds and threw them on the fire. By then Sheriff Bodeen had finished a bottle of whiskey and was hugging everybody, including Chase.

"Son," he said, "you gonna take care'a ma cherished girl or I'm'a gonna bury you in the bayou."

It wasn't exactly congratulations, but Chase knew it was from the heart.

Judge Kelton got crazy on moonshine and started taking off his clothes and chasing Molly Mae around the field. For a girl with some heft to her, she was pretty fleet on her feet. By midafternoon he'd proposed in nothing but his skivvies, and she seemed to be seriously considering it.

She said to Lila, "He's got hisself a fine house, no chilluns, and I hear tell he got money stashed away in mason jars buried 'neath his barn. He gotta be goin' on eighty, I won't have to bear his tomfoolery long."

Lila said, "He's lookin' healthy enough to stay outta the undertaker's clutches a good while longer."

Molly, hitching up her girth. "I reckon I can help him along down that road fast enough."

About sundown the preacher was overcome by another case of the tongues and ran back into the lake. This time Chase let him go. He sat there on the shore beside Lila, her hand in his, watching the preacher call down an army of angels, wondering why Jonah never called, and thinking, Here it is. Here I am.

Chase didn't mind being out of the bent life. Now that he'd gone straight he could use his own name and paperwork again. It had always bothered him he hadn't ever gone to school. He signed up for night classes at a community college sixty miles away and made the trip three times a week in order to earn his GED.

No one in the office ever asked him why he'd quit school in the sixth grade. Even now in Mississippi he wasn't a unique case. If anyone ever got curious, he knew all he had to say was, "Daddy catched ill one winter and I had to take to the fields."

He worked in a local garage doing lube jobs on pickups that smelled like fertilizer and old fish. He took care of their thirty-year-old Chevys that had turned the odometer at least four times. If the cars were dead, he managed to bring them back, if they still had a spark of life, he made them hum. He spent a lot of time fine-tuning the moonrunners' muscle cars, reinforcing the frames so they could take the rutted dirt tracks without bottoming out, even with all the extra weight in the trunk.

Every now and again Bodeen or one of the state troopers would bring their cruisers in for the extra kick Chase could squeeze out of an engine. It quickly got around that he was one of the best mechanics in three states. Bodeen offered him another job as official police mechanic in charge of the auto pool. Chase couldn't help thinking about how easy it would be to gaff all the cars to throw a rod or blow their brake lines on the same night. He could score the whole county while the cops pursued him in flatbeds that couldn't crack forty-five.

Maybe he missed the bent life a little.

Joe-Boo Brinks, the biggest still operator in the area, wanted Chase to come work for him full-time as a mechanic and runner. He tried to woo Chase with the promise of his underage daughter and eighteen grand in cash. He brought the money over in a cardboard suitcase one afternoon while Chase was sitting on a dead log down by the creek having his lunch.

The girl had come along too, wearing a pair of frayed short shorts and a blouse with the sleeves torn off, knotted at her midriff. She had very tight stomach muscles and only a few ounces of baby fat to round her out where it mattered.

Joe-Boo stood six feet of wiry muscle, his mostly bald head gleaming in the sunshine, his graying beard poorly trimmed and sticking out in tufts. A perpetual sour stink wafted off him, part body odor and part sour mash whiskey bleeding from his very pores. He smiled so broadly you could see every empty space and gold tooth in his head, and he repeatedly drew out a red bandana to wipe down his sunburned, freckled crown.

"I put the first set of car keys in the hands of a lot of runners," Joe-Boo told him, "but I ain't never seen anyone drive like you."

"You've never seen me drive, Joe-Boo," Chase said.

"Yeah, I have, when you thought no one lookin'. Out there on the gravel tracks by the river, down near the sweetwater. You go it alone at night, boy, why's that? You could be earnin' money doing the same thing during the day."

"I'm on the narrow, Joe-Boo."

"You ain't always been though, now have you, boy?"

Grabbing hold of his daughter's wrist, Joe-Boo pulled her down beside him and turned her so Chase could take a good look at her ass.

"This here is my youngest, Iris."

"H'lo," Iris said.

Joe-Boo drew her unkempt black hair from her face and she smiled delicately while he did it.

"Don't take but a glance before any man begins to fancy her," Joe-Boo said.

Chase lost his appetite and tossed the uneaten remainder of his lunch back in his brown bag. He

said in a steady voice, "Listen, you're really starting to creep me out, all right? I appreciate the offer but let's just settle on no. You bring your cars in
and I'll fix them up the way I've been doing. For
the rest of it, find another man."

"I need a driver like you, and I aim to get what
I need."

The girl might seem like an empty-headed
backwoods honey, but she was smart enough to
say, "Daddy, let's get on home. He done said no as
nice as he can."

"It's him sayin' yes that I'm after."

"He ain't gonna."

"Hush, baby doll."

With his foot, Joe-Boo shoved the cardboard
suitcase with the money in it closer to Chase. He
was no longer smiling. He'd dropped the neigh-
borly shit and was turning up the heat in his glare.
His eyes were milky and bloodshot. Rumor was
that Joe-Boo carried a switchblade pigsticker and
liked to hurl it into tree trunks from about twenty
yards off. He had fifteen men working under him
in the back hills, and it had taken a lot for him to
walk up bearing cash, showing some respect.

It was an overture not usually made, and Chase
really didn't want to get on the moonshine king's
bad side, but it seemed that was how it was going
to play out.

"You pull that pigsticker and I'm going to have to
shove it up your ass, Joe-Boo," Chase said, shifting
his weight on the log, waiting for Brinks to reach into

his back pocket. "I'm married. You were at my wedding. You've known Lila her whole life. All of you people have known each other your whole lives. Let me tell you something for all our sakes." He leaned in a bit. "She usually drives by the garage about this time every day and comes to sit with me down here at the creek. So let me ask . . . what do you think will happen if she shows up in the next minute or two and spots your cash and your baby girl with her tits practically out, sitting this close to me?"

Joe-Boo Brinks pulled a face, a little pie-eyed now, angry, but the worry leaking into his features ounce by ounce, until he and his daughter finally got the hell out of there.

Chase still liked a little action. That was why he hauled ass down by the gravel tracks. When he felt the urge for a score coming over him he'd scope out a car with a good engine and a solid frame, steal it and tune it up, go for a joyride, and then bring it back in much better condition.

Lila started getting reports from people who picked up on the extra mileage and noticed how fine their engines ran now. Their tires rotated, their plugs changed, timing chains fixed, new air filters and hoses put in.

She would say to him, "You been wheeling around town again? You know what it's going to look like if I have to arrest my own husband?"

"No one's going to press charges because their carburetors were cleaned."

"You never know, and I don't want to have to stick the cuffs back on you."

"You'd have to catch me first."

"That a challenge or a threat?"

"I don't know." He'd take her in his arms and nuzzle her neck. "Which one turns you on more?"

"Both about the same, I'd guess."

He liked to keep up with the boxing to stay fit. He set up a heavy bag, speed bag, and some wrestling mats in the garage. Lila stocked most of her guns out there in a couple of wide lockers that she kept locked. While he worked the bag, skipped rope, or shadowboxed, she'd oil her weapons over on the workbench, pull them apart, and snap them back together. His old burglary tools were wrapped up in a gym bag stashed in the crawl space.

She asked him, "You ever handle a pistol besides mine that night?"

"Not many," he told her. "But I know guns. A couple of guys I used to run with were purveyors. Suppliers, not hitters. They taught me a lot."

"You want to learn about shooting?"

"I think I know all I need to."

"You might be surprised. You're in Mississippi now, sweetness."

"People bleed here if you shoot them in the leg

just like they do anywhere else. I'm almost sure I've seen a practical demonstration of that someplace."

"I reckon I recall seeing something along those lines myself."

She didn't push any further although he knew that his hatred for firearms ran counter to everything she knew. Her father had taught her how to shoot when she was three—goddamn three. But between his mother's murder and having seen Jonah tapping Walcroft, he had an aversion that almost bordered on phobia.

He was a driver. No driver he'd ever heard about carried a gun, at least not on the job. A wheelman sat in the car, kept his nerve, and waited for his crew even as the alarms went off and the sirens whipped closer.

After he'd finished his workout he stood there pouring sweat, watching her while she finished cleaning her .38. He reached around her and picked up the bottle of gun oil and said, "This have any other uses?"

"Hell, we got us some cherry, cinnamon, and scented oils for just those kind of improper thoughts and unsavorish doings."

"I don't remember the cinnamon."

"No? It was a wedding present from Judge Kelton."

He frowned and licked his teeth, the taste already in his mouth, and said, "If you don't ever want my mood to sink, please don't tell me things like that."

"Just give me a minute to put my sidearm away

and we'll work on that sinking mood, see if we can't elevate it some."

"I have complete faith," he said, and it turned out not to be misplaced.

Another time, she stood in the center of the mats and said, "You want I should show you some moves?"

"I've got the moves, thank you anyway."

"Ain't talking about those, which are adequate at best."

"Hey, now—"

"I'm talking about these."

She got behind him, reached forward and wrapped her right arm around his neck, thrust his chin aside with the back of her hand, and flipped him backward over her hip. He rose five feet into the air and came down flat on his back. It stunned him and his head swam. She got on top of him, turned him over, cuffed him, and pinned him so he couldn't breathe. With his vision starting to go black at the edges, maybe five or ten seconds from passing out, she finally climbed off.

He lay there groaning for a while until he got his breath back. He realized, with a swelling sadness, that somewhere inside her she resented how their first meeting had gone—if he hadn't gotten the drop on her, she would've kicked his ass. He sputtered and gasped. "You really think I'm only adequate?"

"But with a touch of potential in some areas," she said, and left him cuffed on the mat while she

yanked down his sweatpants and took degenerate
advantage of him.

After a year of trying, they drove up to St. Louis to
see a specialist. The tests included a lot of unholy
acts against him, Chase thought, including the
forced and unnatural congress with a Dixie cup,
but when he complained about these misdeeds
against his flesh Lila got the giggles so bad she
nearly flopped off the chair.

Easy for her to dismiss. But getting your
prostate checked at twenty-one was bound to make
any guy a little distressed. He was hoping to hold
off that particularly disconcerting and downright
unflattering situation until he was at least fifty, and
maybe even then he'd balk.

"There's going to be an accounting for this," he
said. "If not in this life, then the next."

"You never got this edgy being the wheelman
for a diamond heist."

"You've got to draw your lines somewhere."

"You don't know what true invasion is," she
said. "Until your ankles are locked in stirrups and
a geezer with a flashlight and a speculum has
crawled eight inches up into your belly."

"Jesus Christ, this I need to hear?" He didn't
even want to know what a speculum was.

"It'll help you to appreciate the life you lead."

"I appreciate it plenty," he said, and he meant it.
After a second visit, the specialist with the fuck-

ing frigid fingers narrowed down the problem to Lila. Chase tried to follow the biology behind it, but for a guy who'd never made it past the sixth grade, he was having trouble visualizing things, and the doctor wasn't using a pointer to tap on the chart on his wall the way Chase had been hoping.

The doc said it wasn't impossible, but the odds were significantly narrower for Lila than the "average young female" to become pregnant and carry a child full-term.

She said, "Well, I was raised to believe in miracles."

When they got home she unloaded two hundred rounds into the woods, trying to snuff ghosts.

Chase tried to keep Lila laughing because he knew it was starting to get to her, the fact that what came naturally to everyone else wasn't happening for them. All day long they'd see pregnant teenagers heading to Mrs. Haskins's Home for Wayward Unwed Girls & Peanut Farm. Lila had something like nineteen uncles and aunts, thirty-seven cousins, her parents, and both sets of grandparents living less than five miles away. At every family function they all let her have it. Asking when she was going to have a kid.

It worked her nerves. Chase knew they all figured he must have bad genes, being a Yankee and now this, and he let them keep on believing it. Lila cared and he didn't.

She hung in there, but on certain nights the fact rattled her and a black mood would hit. She'd hold him tightly as if he might be running out on her, really putting her weight into it and using some cop holds on him, twisting him down. With her mascara running she'd say, "I'm so sorry."

"There's nothing to be sorry about."

"There is."

No matter what he said he couldn't snap her out of it. She had to bounce back on her own. They'd lie there drinking wine or whiskey, the heavy breeze coming down out of the hills washing the curtains back.

She only brought up his parents or Jonah when the idea of motherhood started to drift away from her. "You think he ever loved you? Your grand-daddy?"

"Yes," Chase said, surprising both of them.

"You loved him?"

"Yes."

"But you were afraid of him."

"Everybody was afraid of him."

"And you just couldn't trust him anymore after that last card game."

"Even before that. He would've thrown me over if he had to. I just thought I'd be the last one he threw over." Chase sipped the whiskey. "It's part of the way the pros do things."

"Leaving their friends behind?"

"Yeah," he admitted. "If there's no other way around it."

"But you didn't. Not the night we met. You hung around. You never ran."

"No, I don't run."

"A' course, you did wind up shooting your own string."

"Only in their legs. And only for you."

"Wasn't much of a getaway."

"It was for you."

"So warm, sweetness," she said and rolled to him. "I bet the other girls just got flowers and chocolates."

Chase began dreaming of his mother and the dead little sibling, the one who hadn't had a chance to be born. He'd spent years trying to forget her face, tamping those memories down inside him, but now she appeared before him quite clearly, her voice almost breezy as she spoke his name.

He was back in the house he grew up in. The lawn had been mowed, the edging along the grass done with precision, the hedges perfectly trimmed, the tops as straight as if they'd been laid out with a ruler. Either it was high aesthetic or his father had a touch of OCD.

At the kitchen table, his mother sat calling to him, as if he was in another room. He stepped closer but she couldn't seem to see him. He noted the way she wore her hair in looping ringlets, a slight reddish tint to it, the same as he got in his beard when he let it grow out. Her lips were

full, almost as full as Lila's. Her belly just a tiny
bulge.

He waited to see himself, as a boy, come running by, but it didn't happen. The dead little kid
was in a chair at the other end of the table. Weird
to see it and still not know if it was a boy or a girl.
It stared at him with its mouth moving, indeci-
pherable sounds emerging and growing louder
until he thought he could almost make them out.
He moved closer and closer, and the kid leaned
forward and spit in his face.

I dreamed of my mother again last night," Chase
told her.

"I thought you might be," Lila said. "The way
you twisted in your sleep. I held you and rubbed
your chest lightly and you quieted down some after a time."

She'd been raised on mountain folklore, backwoods myths, and gospel tent revivals. No matter
how hard she tried, she'd never be able to lose the
superstitious streak that had been spiked into her
from childhood. When he spoke of his dreams her
face grew very intense and she spooked him a little
with how seriously she took them.

"What did your mama tell you?" she asked.

"Nothing. She just kept saying my name."

Lila nodded, like spirits did this on occasion.
He wondered if he should go fire a few rounds
into the woods, maybe it would ease his mind a bit.

Lila studied him for a moment, her features folding along all the contours of worry. It made his guts tighten, and she laid a hand against the side of his face.

"The dead will find a way to you. They'll make you listen."

It took about four years in Mississippi before he started to lose his cool. He'd done pretty well, all things considered.

They were at a picnic on a lake, all the kids running around down by the shore, skimming rocks and chasing turtles. Molly Mae and Judge Kelton had three little ones by now and were working on a fourth, the old man getting healthier by the year while Molly looked ready to throw herself under a truck.

Chase tried to keep his mind on the conversations circling him, but the accent still threw him off and he laughed inappropriately on occasion. He was never going to get a handle on it.

He knew he'd been getting a little distant and didn't know how to bring himself back.

Lila came over and sat on his lap. "You want to head home to the East Coast, don't you."

"Yes."

He knew she wanted to leave this place, maybe even more than he did, just to get away from the constant reminder of her family asking about when they were going to have children.

"You think I'll like it there?" she asked.

"It'll take some adjustment, but yeah, I think you will."

"We going to live in Manhattan? I'm not sure I could get used to a big city like that."

"You could, but I think we'll be better off out on Long Island. Get a little house."

"I suppose police work would be a little more action-packed."

It made him tense up. He hadn't thought for a minute she'd want to stay a cop in New York.

"I don't think that's an especially good idea," he said.

Her voice grew heavy as she whispered into his ear. "You think those bad New York crews are going to take advantage of my poor countrified ways?"

"You wouldn't be out there arresting your cousin Ernie."

"Now you know Ernie was a real villain despite him being blood."

It was supposed to make him feel like an idiot but instead it alarmed him a touch. She was strong and smart and could handle herself, but New York was a different world from anything she'd known. He thought about trying to talk her out of it, making a real scene if he had to, but there wasn't any point. She'd hold her course the way she always had, right from the start.

Lila had never seen the ocean before. The first thing he did was take her down to the beaches. The water hypnotized her, the ever-shifting terrain and form of it, the endless blue and white fading beyond the vanishing point of the horizon. It took her hours before she went in up to her ankles. The sea terrified and elated her. A couple of times she kneeled and splashed, as if she were playing with a child. The waves rolled in and out, and from second to second, as her eyes widened and narrowed, it appeared to Chase that she had to force herself to remember she didn't have a lost child rolling in the surf. That the kid had never been there no matter how alive in her mind it might be, calling out to her.

He became a teacher, like his father, in a town not far from where he grew up and where his mother had been murdered. Auto shop. He didn't need a master's degree to show kids how to fix a fan belt. Most of them couldn't even change a spark plug and were only there because the other elective in the time slot was Home Ec. What you wound up with was all the girls learning how to make waffles and all the guys trying to act manly even though they each had Triple A and would call a towing service before changing a tire.

Only a handful of the boys were destined to be grease monkeys. They didn't have the grades or the attitude for college and were bound to work in garages for the rest of their lives. A couple would take to it, and the others would probably be hissing in bitterness for decades to come. Chase taught them all the way Jonah and a few of the other string members had taught him, as if there was something mythic and lifesaving hidden within the depths of a car.

The kids liked him because he was young and cared more about life lessons than he did about grades. He'd watch them in the hallways and listen to their chatter. So many of them seemed bent out of shape already, worried about college, their résumés, mortgages they didn't even have yet. He was astonished by the number of kids who had to go to rehab, had psychiatrists, took antidepressants because they'd already tried to off themselves. For the first time he started to realize maybe he'd been better off without school after all.

He taught the kids a couple of car-boosting tricks. Nothing too serious, just goofing around. But it solidified his reputation. They dug the way he spoke to them, as equals. Unlike other teachers, Chase would never judge or analyze them, and the kids knew it. The rest of the faculty members, trying to relate, would have to sift back through their lives and make an effort to recall what it was like to be a teen.

But they couldn't quite remember and they didn't really want to. It was too painful. Resentment would flare. So they wound up looking fake and deceptive despite their sincerity. He saw it happening all the time. Watching some old man make an ass out of himself hoping to sound hip, waving hall passes around, throwing a conniption fit if anyone was still around after the bell rang.

But Chase had never been a kid and had never been to school. He couldn't pretend even if he wanted to. He talked to his students the way he talked to everyone. They respected him for it. They also knew that if they ever crossed him or gave him too much shit, he wouldn't send them to the principal's office. He'd take care of it himself. It kept them on their toes.

Despite already being a deputy sheriff, Lila had to pay for a couple of academy courses and wound up a Suffolk County cop, which was considered a cush job by the New York City fuzz. She said some of the guys gave her a hard time because of her accent, but she liked her partner, a kid a few years younger than her named Hopkins, and so far there hadn't been too much rough action.

Hopkins was married and had two baby daughters. He and his wife came over for cake and coffee— that's what you were supposed to do here, married couples, have cake and coffee—and brought the kids with them. Lila left Chase in the kitchen having the fucking cake and coffee while she played with the girls in the other room the whole time. He didn't blame her, but hell, enough with the cake and coffee.

Lila told him, "Maybe you should quit teaching them kids how to steal cars. Since you started in on their fertile minds, joyriding in the area's gone up about three thousand percent."

She was too damn good at her job, giving the guys on the force a complex. Always getting citations, commendations, and medals for something or other. There were plenty of photo ops, the chief of her division and other public servants standing beside her, smiling, sometimes holding their hands up in a salute. It didn't hurt to get your photo in the paper next to a beautiful young woman. Chase figured they got a little extra thrill pinning the medal to her chest, going in for a quick grope. They'd put one hand on her shoulder and the other on her ass. He noted their faces.

On occasion, she'd have some kind of a banquet or police ceremony to attend and he'd get a free dinner out of it. When the gropers came around to shake his hand, telling him what a fine officer his wife was, the pride of the order, Chase would pretend to trip and give them a cheap shot to the kidneys. It wasn't much but you retaliated where you could. The Jonah in his head told him to carry a roll of quarters in his fist next time.

Eventually it got back to the PTA that Chase was teaching the kids how to boost rides and he was brought up for review. He sat there in a classroom that had been set up to look like a court, with the judge behind the desk and him in a little chair off on his own. He got scolded by a couple of tight-asses, and he had to promise not to do it anymore. The whole review board thing didn't carry much weight anyway since he was consistently voted one of the most popular teachers in the school district.

Sometimes at night he felt a little guilty stealing Lila away from the life she had always known before. He held her tightly with his face pressed between her breasts, breathing deeply, and she brushed her fingers through his hair and said, "You don't have anything to feel conscience-struck about. I love it here. You gave me the ocean."

"Is it enough?"

"Nothing is except for you, love. You're enough. And that's all that matters." She kissed him and looked into his eyes, going deep again, the way she did. "'Sides, if we'd stayed in Mississippi, I'd be babysitting. Molly Mae just had her sixth."

"Jesus Christ, six! How's the judge?"

"He's ready to walk on water, that miraculous sumbitch."

They hit the city, and Lila fell in love with Broadway.

So did Chase, all over again. Back when he was pulling heists with Jonah just outside of the city, he'd managed to take in a number of shows during their downtime, the scheme time. None of these major musicals playing in the elaborate theaters, but the classics held in smaller 99-seat venues. Chekhov's *The Cherry Orchard*, Ibsen's *Ghosts*, Albee's *A Delicate Balance*, and an all-female version of Beckett's *Waiting for Godot*. He was only fourteen but had appreciated them greatly, as they stirred him toward understanding metaphor and sentiment. He even caught a revival of Shaffer's *Equus* and was surprised to see nudity on the stage. He'd been embarrassed as hell, slinking down in his seat with his cheeks heating up.

He and Lila started going to the theater as often as they could afford it. Prices were outrageous, and he didn't know how the other stiffs managed to swing the shows. Two tickets, dinner, and parking ran upwards of three or four bills, but they managed to make a night of it at least once a month, so long as Lila wasn't pulling night shifts.

One evening, after *The Producers,* which Lila found hysterical and Chase thought was way too broadly acted, they were walking down Seventh Avenue toward a little Italian place they liked when a guy bumped into Chase and said, "'Scuse me, buddy."

"Sure," Chase said, knowing something had just gone wrong. It took him a second to check his wallet.

Gone. His pocket had been picked.

Goddamn, that had been a nice brazen, fluid move. A quick dip, lift, and fly. The straight life had made him careless. Getting hit by a nimble, practiced pickpocket, it actually surprised him the way it would a regular citizen. Chase wasn't sure if he should rush after the mook or ask Lila to go grab him, use her wily police skills all over his ass.

"What's wrong?" she asked.

"I just had my wallet lifted."

"You know by who?"

Chase still had his eye on the guy up ahead in the foot traffic. "Yeah."

"Well? You gonna let him get away with the

boodle? Or you want I should do all the work even on my night off?"

"You are the defender of the peace," Chase said. "My taxes pay your salary."

"I'm simply a wife expecting to be treated to a nice dinner in a fancy restaurant."

"Be right back."

"Don't take too long, I'm jonesing for some lasagna."

Pronouncing it la-zanga.

"Get a bottle of Merlot and order me the fettuccine Alfredo," Chase said and took off down Seventh Avenue after the pickpocket, weaving through the crowd.

He found the guy zipping around the corner, heading for a subway station. Walking hurriedly but without breaking into a run. He was good but not especially smart. He should've stayed with the street crowd instead of taking the corner and making for a subway fifteen minutes before the next train. He should've had the cash out by now and dumped the wallet.

Chase got up close behind the mook, invading space, and made the guy stop and turn around to see who was breathing down his neck. No one else was nearby.

"I'm curious," Chase said, "what made you choose me?"

"What?"

Up close, the stealthy mutt didn't blend in with

the urban hordes as much as Chase had originally thought. He was only around thirty but already seriously burned at the edges. Wrinkled, faded, and losing the fight to keep from being swept out to sea. A cokehead but not overly wired at the moment, his eyes a low grade of lethal. What Jonah used to call a skel, a dreg, a bottom-feeder.

"I'm no mark," Chase told him. "Your kind always go after the tourist trade and folks who are distracted or lost. So why me?"

"What?"

Okay, so no reminiscing over the bent life with this one. Chase would have to settle on getting just a brief whiff of the old days. "Give me my wallet."

"Get the fuck away. I don't know what you're talking about."

"Sure you do. Come on, let's have it."

"You don't want a piece of me."

"You've got that right. Just hand over my wallet."

"I'm not kidding with you, man, go back to fucking Kentucky or wherever you're from."

Now that was just mean-spirited. "New York born and bred, fucker!"

The guy drew his chin to his chest, eyes narrowing, squeezing out the world. He went deep, calling up anger and hate and letting it wash over him. You could see it happening, how the guy was just letting himself go, drifting with the worst that was inside him. All of this for what? Chase had maybe eighty bucks in the wallet, two credit cards he could cancel in sixty seconds.

But the mook had skilled hands all right. One second there was nothing in his fist, and the next he was holding a fold-out blade. It snapped open with a dramatic click. Chase hadn't been expecting a blade or pistol. Most pickpockets went into the trade because of its relative safety. No confrontation, no muscle, nobody gets hurt. No weapons were used so any jail time was light.

But this one, he'd worked a lot with his knife. Maybe it was the coke. It kept him up three days straight with nothing to do but practice.

He kept the blade down low, out straight before him. He did everything right so far as Chase knew. A couple of strings he'd been a part of had had knife fighters on them. Guys who did nothing but sharpen blades and throw them into dartboards between scores. Almost all of them went down after carving up someone in a barroom brawl.

You saw a guy with a knife in this day and age and you knew you were looking at a serious asshole.

The mutt unleashed a nice speedy move, and suddenly the knife was coming in at a nasty angle. None of this slashing shit, not even the usual stabbing motion. A low-slung swinging arc coming up from the groin. If it hooked into Chase's belly it would yank out his guts.

The fuck was wrong with these antisocial sons

of bitches? You could rob a man without butchering him.

Chase barely avoided the maneuver, got his left arm up to block and shot off two rapid-fire punches to the guy's nose. It brought blood but didn't slow the mook down any. He made another low, slicing action.

"You're fast but you don't know when to call it quits," Chase said.

The guy was too focused to respond, on a complete burn with his heart rate up. He looked like he just didn't give a damn about anything anymore, like he might as well kill or die as soon as walk away.

Chase was only twenty-five and in prime shape, but the straight life had worn him down a little, made him soft. He saw what might happen. Imagined himself snuffed on the curb, with Lila eating breadsticks for the next hour thinking what the hell had happened to him, and wondering when she could crack the wine and get some pasta.

"Shit," Chase said.

The blade came upward toward Chase's groin and he caught the guy's wrist, squeezed and bent it back, feeling the little bones grind into sand. The knife dropped and clattered on the cement. Chase tugged forward and sidestepped. The mook let loose with an outraged yelp as he passed by Chase's shoulder, the light stir of breeze sort of singing, and Chase spun and elbowed him hard in the back of the head.

The pickpocket went down like he was dead.

Bathed in cold sweat, Chase staggered against the side of a building, gasping for air. It took him a minute to get back his cool. He went through the mutt's pockets. Tore open a folded envelope and poured out a gram of coke on the sidewalk. Found a tightly rolled wad of eleven hundred bucks and took it. Got his wallet and five others. Another grand or so, not including his own eighty bucks. He pocketed it all.

Fuck off for the night, straight life.

Turning the corner, he found a mailbox and tossed the other wallets in.

At the restaurant, Lila had already ordered and was digging into a plate of lasagna, a hunk of buttered bread on the side of her plate, an open bottle of Merlot in the center of the table. God he loved to see her eat. His fettuccine was still steaming. Perfect timing. He sat and poured two glasses, downed his own quickly, and poured another.

She said, "Go wash, there's blood on your hands."

He hadn't noticed. It took him a minute in the men's room to scrub a stain out of his cuff. He knew she'd never ask him anything about it, giving him plenty of room to move. When he got back, the waiter was passing by, and Chase ordered Dom Pérignon.

She said, "Champagne?"

Why the hell not, he was twenty-one big ones ahead. "It's a celebration."

"My. And just what are we celebrating, sweet-ness?"

"That you're not a widow," Chase told her.

They went to another specialist at the Center for Human Reproduction in Manhasset. A real fat cat who blinked and sniffed a lot. This time the doc had a big chart on a wall and he drew on it with an erasable marker, showing the ins and outs of all their plumbing. Chase was a little sorry he'd been given the grand tour. Of all the mysteries that needed to be solved, he figured this one was better left in the shadows of the bedroom. The doc told him to wear boxers. Chase hated boxers but he'd been wearing them for years, since the first specialist told him to wear boxers. The doc gave him pills so he could power up the little guys and get them to do their business despite the hardships they faced.

In the deep night, when she thought he was asleep, Lila would whisper that she was sorry. But he wasn't sure she was saying it to him. Just putting it out there to the universe. Sometimes he just let her talk, and sometimes he'd feel the need to tell her it wasn't her fault. He'd fight for the light, but by the time he got the lamp on she'd be pretending to be asleep.

Chase got a call from Hopkins saying Lila had taken a wrench to the back while busting up a roadside car lot in Wyandanch.

Hopkins described the scam even though Chase already knew it. He'd been the one to explain it to Lila, who'd then told Hopkins.

Failing auto shops would partner up for a hit. Clean out the garages and claim that all their tools and cars brought in for servicing had been stolen. They'd put in insurance claims and shut their doors. One day there'd be a thriving auto shop on the corner, and the next everything was wiped clean, not even a can of motor oil left behind. The cars would be sold off cheap at a highway rest stop or a corner lot someplace, mostly to old men who knew the score and didn't care or teenagers who'd learn fast the first time they caught a ticket.

Whatever didn't sell in twelve hours was taken to a chop shop. After the insurance came through, a new garage opened up across town, with all the same tools and stock, and everybody would take their part of the kick.

Lila mentioned the trouble they were having in the Wyandanch–Deer Park area and Chase told her exactly how the scam worked. Three days later, she and Hopkins went out and caught one of the roadside lots going full swing. They got into a high-speed pursuit with the guys running the show, racing down the Sagtikos to Ocean Parkway. Lila always drove. She'd learned a lot from Chase over the years. She rammed the getaway car and nearly drove it off the Robert Moses Bridge into the Great South Bay.

They arrested a trio of perps right there on the bridge. While Hopkins was reading them their Miranda, a skinny guy with a lot of grease on his hands managed to slip his cuffs and come at Lila with a twelve-inch crescent wrench he'd hidden down the back of his overalls.

Doesn't look like much until you get hit with it. That fucker can powder bones.

At the hospital, the doctors told Chase there was nerve damage and pressure on her spine. She couldn't feel her legs. They weren't sure if she'd ever walk again.

In her hospital bed she laughed it off while he tried to shake his terror and smile at her. She said, "'A' course I'm gonna walk again, the hell kinda foolishness is that? I'm just a little bruised."

Turned out she was right. Not even twelve hours later she was up and walking around, feeling fine. The goddamn doctors, they'd give you their very worst right out of the gate just so you couldn't come back at them later with a lawsuit for building up your hopes. Still, they wanted her to stay put for observation.

Chase called Deucie, who was still running the same chop shop for the mob in Jersey. He said, "There's a crew working the roadside car lot scam in Wyandanch."

"What do I care about fucking Long Island?" the Deuce said.

"They've lost three of their main guys in charge of the show. It's going to take them a while to get reorganized and figure out what to do with all the product the cops haven't already seized. Anybody with a little resolve and muscle can take over a couple of garages worth of stock, autos, and car parts."

"I'll think about it."

Sure he would. A couple of days later a string of auto shops in the area went out of business and never did reopen across town. Chase called Deucie back, said, "Okay, now I need something."

"Of course you do. This got anything to do with the mutt who beat up your old lady?"

It snapped Chase's chin up, hearing it laid down like that. He didn't know Deucie would've checked him out so thoroughly. "Yeah."

The Deuce made a noise, a kind of snorting laugh.

"What?" Chase asked.

"It's what Jonah would do."

"Fuck that noise, Deuce. Jonah would do it himself. So listen, you got anybody who knows anybody who's stuck out at the Suffolk County lockup?"

"Not any of those short-time local inmates, but I think I have a friend who knows a correctional guard."

The guy with the crescent wrench's name was Cordell Williams. Chase had been turning the name around and around in his head. He said, "He'll be getting transferred to Rikers soon."

"And before he does? You want him aced? That's going to cost you more than some cheap-shit car wrecks and a couple dozen boxed mufflers."

"I just want him worked over enough that he lays in bed for a while and reflects on his life's mistakes."

"You always were a little soft."

"Call me when it's done."

The Deuce phoned the next afternoon. "They put the hurt on him. Busted a couple of ribs, three or four of his toes. Hope that's not too rough for you."

Chase thought it was a little light but said, "Fine."

Her first day home, lying on the couch with a bunch of satin pillows propped behind her, she got a call from Hopkins. He must've told her about what had happened to Cordell Williams, but she just hung up, flipped on the television, and started watching some cooking show. If she suspected Chase had anything to do with it, she never said a word to him about it. But once, during a commercial, he caught her grinning at him.

A couple of months later her parents came in for a weeklong visit during Lila's vacation. Chase picked them up at Newark and played tour guide, showing them some of Manhattan. Passing by the Empire State Building, Rockefeller Center, Radio City Music Hall. He crawled up Fifth Avenue pointing out the Metropolitan Museum of Art, Museum Mile, the Guggenheim. Right from the start they were both withdrawn and spooked. The traffic terrified them, the noise, the smell. He figured he'd botched the mission by killing them with culture shock on their first day in town, and he got them back to his house as fast as he could.

Lila had an itinerary: barbecue that afternoon. Head out to Montauk Point the next day, go see the seals. Later in the week, go take in a Broadway show, visit to the top of the Empire State Building, do the Circle Line, see the Statue of Liberty.

But Chase had blown it. There, fifteen minutes after her parents set foot in the living room, both he and Lila realized none of it was ever going to happen. They grilled steaks in the backyard for five days straight.

Sheriff Bodeen sat on the patio chair and drank a case of beer a day. Watched a lot of television, commented on the state of the front lawn, and cleaned Lila's already extremely clean guns. And every afternoon, when Chase got home from work, Bodeen found the need to ask him, "So when you gonna put my little gal in a family way?"

The week crawled by like a gutted animal. Chase started staying at the school later and later, even after everyone had gone except for him and the janitors. The custodial staff played their radios and buffed the floors, and Chase would sit in the automotive shop pulling out and rebuilding transmissions for the hell of it.

At the end of the week, Lila's mother, the quietest woman Chase had ever met, hugged him good-bye, squeezing hard and putting all her burly muscle into it, said, "When you gonna put my little gal in a family way?"

They went to another specialist in Manhattan. This one doused any last hope. He looked at the files and charts and focused his attention entirely on Lila, explaining why she couldn't get pregnant, patting her lightly on the shoulder and running his hand down the back of her hair, flattening it with his hesitant touch. He occasionally pressed his fingers to her belly, drawing little maps of where her internal organs were. Which ones were doing their job, which ones weren't. When he jabbed at the offending parts of her anatomy, Lila's face would darken. He told them that miracles were always possible, and he said it like they'd have to be fucking idiots to believe it. He walked out without another word.

No one else would've noticed the shift in her expression. In every way it appeared to be the same as before the doc had entered the little room and poked at her and said his piece, but Chase saw a world of difference. She wouldn't want to break down in front of him, but it was an hour's train ride back to their station on Long Island. He didn't think she'd be able to make it.

They took a cab to Penn and he felt the guilt and remorse within her straining to break free, the small space separating them in the backseat filled as if by the presence of a remote but solidifying dream. He didn't suggest adoption because he knew that, more than wanting to bear a child, she wanted to bear his child. She'd always hoped to offer Chase the stability of the healthy, happy family he'd never had growing up. No matter how often he told her that it was all right with him, she wouldn't accept it. It was just another reason to love her.

*   *   *

They entered Penn Station from Seventh Avenue and moved quickly down two flights of stairs to the Long Island Railroad waiting room. They had almost a half hour before their train and he decided to give her a few minutes alone to cry in the ladies' room if she needed to.

He asked if she wanted anything and she told him to get a slice of pizza for her. Italian food was the one thing she loved better than Southern cooking. They had pizza three times a week. He didn't mind, he'd been missing it badly for years, and it reminded him of Friday nights when he was a kid and his father would bring a pie home for dinner.

He had to fight the rush-hour throng to make it to the parlor on the other side of the station. The place was crowded and he hung back waiting a few minutes until he thought she might be through with her crying jag. He ordered four slices and a couple of sodas and carried them back to the waiting room.

Three cops were there waving their billy clubs in the air, and Lila had her knee on some guy's throat. He was a well-trimmed youth in a camouflage jacket, his mouth bleeding and his face going purple while he struggled to breathe. He wasn't having much luck with it since Lila was kind of crushing his thorax. Her purse was on the floor beside her with a few bills on the loose.

Chase quickly put together what must've happened. The kid asking for spare change, Lila handing him a dollar, and then the punk making a grab for the wallet.

She was saying, "If your mama ain't learned you no manners, then maybe the fine gentlemen at Rikers Island will!" When she was pissed her accent came on even stronger. "You goin' to see what they there charge you for lessons in flesh and bone, boy!"

With every word she nudged up and down on his neck and he went "Gug!"

The cops finally wrestled her off and nearly arrested her until she flashed her badge. They hauled the punk off, she gave her statement and signed the papers. It had all taken less than ten minutes.

Chase stood there as she stepped over and took the bagged pizza from him. "I'm a damn sight on the far side of hungry, sweetness," she said, tearing into a slice. "Bless yer soul."

It rained like a son of a bitch the day she died.

He was showing the kids how to flush a transmission and do a fluid change when one of the math teachers appeared at the door. He called Chase aside. He'd been on break in the parking lot, smoking a cigarette listening to his car radio, and told him what he'd just heard. The breaking news report hadn't mentioned any names, but when they said a female police officer had been taken in for emergency surgery after a shoot-out at a diamond wholesaler in Hauppauge, he thought he'd better tell Chase.

Chase kept his cell phone turned off during class hours. He snapped it on and checked the messages. There was one from Hopkins. Chase could barely make out what the fuck he was saying due to all the sirens in the background. Hopkins was crying.

Taking flooded corners at seventy, Chase got to the hospital in fifteen minutes and parked in the red zone. It was coming down so hard that the twenty-yard dash to the door left him completely drenched. He spotted Hopkins beating the shit out of a coffee machine. Chase walked past, found a nurse, and gave her Lila's name.

The nurse scuttled off and came back with a young doctor who needed to work on his people skills. The guy blurted out that Lila had taken a bullet in the throat and two in the chest, one nicking her heart. Thirty seconds later, as an addendum with artificial syrup dripped on, he stated how they'd tried their best, *their very best,* but there was really nothing anyone could do. It was her time. The young doctor licked his teeth like he smelled sirloin. His black hair was moussed with the front swirled into a little curtain of tight, dyed-blond ringlets that wasn't marred by any breaking sweat. Chase asked if she was DOA.

No, the doc said, no. No. She'd died on the table. He told Chase where to go if he wanted to see the body.

The body.

He didn't. He put the flat of his hand on the doc's chest and shoved him away. The guy fell back into the nurses' station and almost said something. How smart of him not to.

There was blood in the air. Some of it Lila's, none of it Chase's. Think about the mistake of that.

Chase dove for the cold spot and couldn't seem

to find it. It had moved from the place where it had always been before. Seconds ticked off like lifetimes going by as he kept seeking the spot and coming up empty. Finally he realized he was already there.

It was a deeper and blacker place than he remembered, but the ice slid over his utter desolation, cooling him, forcing him to function. Chase asked what caliber the bullets had been, and the doctor just looked at him. The storm tore at the windows. Chase repeated himself and the doc lurched backward.

Nothing more out of that one. Chase turned and Hopkins's wife was there sobbing in the hallway. So was Hopkins, the two of them staggering around together, not quite touching for a minute, and then finally grasping hold of each other. Hospital security was yelling about the busted coffee machine. Hopkins's hands were badly skinned, blood leaking onto the floor. Hopkins and his wife went to their knees. Nothing out of them either.

They didn't notice Chase until he was almost to the door and then they started calling to him, his own name sailing past. He didn't look back.

PART

III

Her parents refused to come up to New York and Sheriff Bodeen insisted that Chase ship Lila's body back to Mississippi. The man's voice was empty of strength. He sounded halfway to being dead himself. Chase said he'd get it done after the service the Suffolk County Police Department wanted to have since she was killed in the line of duty. Sheriff Bodeen dropped the phone and started weeping. Hester got on and said more to Chase right then than she'd said during the five years he'd lived down the road from her in Mississippi.

It was all ugly. Chase listened and absorbed every curse and caterwaul. He promised to send her body back. He didn't know how the fuck something like that was done, but he'd find out and get it accomplished. He knew he'd never see the Bodeens again. He tried to find it within himself to care—losing these people, his in-laws, Lila's mama

and daddy—but it just wasn't there. He hung up
and they were gone from him too.

He slept in fits. He'd wake up from a deep sleep
with a noise so loud in his head that he had to
press his hands over his ears.

It was the sound Walcroft made after Jonah had
shot him in the head. It went on and on, growing
louder as it came down through the years to find
him.

After the big police production where they played
taps and fired their rifles in the air, wearing their
fancy gear and little white gloves, with a huge
photo of Lila's face on an easel beside her casket,
Chase shook hands with the mayor and took the
folded flag they shoved at him, and stood there
while they all got in their photo ops. They talked
at him for hours and he just nodded when he
thought it was appropriate. Sometimes it was and
sometimes it wasn't. Sometimes they frowned at
him or shook him by the arm.

A lot of cops came up and said how much they
admired Lila. Students and teachers and lunch-
room attendants took his hand and tried to make
him feel better by talking about peace and para-
dise, telling him to put his faith in God's wis-
dom and justice. Before it was all over Chase had

given the flag away to somebody, he didn't know who.

He had to shift gears quickly, get back up to speed.

Two days later, when Lila's body was on the plane heading back to her parents, he called Hopkins at home and said, "I want whatever you've got on the ice knockoff."

Hopkins went, "The what?"

The Suffolk cops really *did* have a cush job. So cush they didn't know the language of action. "The diamond merchant score. I need whatever paperwork you have. I want you to tell me everything. In detail."

"Christ, no."

"I have to know what happened that day. From the beginning."

Hopkins started crying again. Chase hated the sound of it, but let him sob, knowing that in some way, great or small, Hopkins had been in love with Lila. He'd felt protective of her, responsible for her, and buoyed by her. Chase couldn't fault the guy for that. He waited until Hopkins got a grip, blew his nose, and cleared his throat. Then he broke down again. Chase waited.

Finally Hopkins said, "We don't allow that."

Chase let it slide. "Who's in charge of the case?"

"Detectives Murray and Morgan."

"Out of your precinct?"

"Yeah. Listen to me, about Lila—"

Chase listened and Hopkins said nothing. He asked, "Well, what about her?"

"I mean, I just wanted to say—" The cop's voice was tight, and he was about to let go again. He'd never swing a full twenty and make his pension. Chase wondered what Hopkins's wife thought, having to listen to this, her husband weeping every time Lila's name came up. "She was a good woman, a good cop, you know, I thought I should—"

Chase hung up and drove over to the station. He asked for Detectives Murray and Morgan and got pointed to the squad room.

Turned out they were two old-school hard-asses, thick and gray, who didn't like to deal with civilians. They must've remembered Chase from the funeral and tried to commiserate with him in that silent *mano a mano* sharing-the-rough-times vibe bullshit. They'd been at this for so long they didn't feel anything anymore, and could barely make the effort to pretend to. They didn't bother to work hard at placating him, just acted as if they deserved to throw off attitude because they were the good guys. As if cops feel pain deeper than the rest of the world. They kept calling him Mister and making it sound like Fuck off, twinky. Chase wondered what it would do to other men who'd recently lost their wives, being forced to deal with these two heartless pricks.

He smiled pleasantly and thanked them for their time.

For two hours he parked out front waiting until Murray and Morgan took off for lunch. Chase walked back inside the squad room, acted like he had a right to be there, and squirreled around Morgan's and Murray's desk drawers until he found the right files and a copy of the security tape.

Police precincts have the worst security in the world. It was no surprise their evidence rooms were always being ripped off from either the inside or the outside.

As he was walking away, a cop coming from the other direction gave him the stink-eye and said, "Can I help you with something?"

Chase said, "Nope," trying hard to make it sound like Fuck off, twinky, and walked out.

A pro job all the way. Four-man string. A diamond wholesaler in Hauppauge. Three inside and the driver not far from the Court building. Chase could imagine the crew having a nice chuckle over that.

He watched the clock in the corner of the tape. In and out in exactly three minutes. One guy watching the employees, another going after the cases in front, a third in the back room clearing out uncut stones. They wore ski masks and black clothing to eliminate any descriptive details. They carried heavy artillery, looked like Colt Pythons. Serious hardware.

He watched the tape again. One of the female employees mouthed off and a gunman shoved her hard against a wall, threatening her with the four-inch barrel in her face. A male employee jumped up and said something and got smashed across the nose for it. Blood spurted and he dropped to the floor, holding his face and rocking.

Only a couple of witnesses had seen the get-away car. They all agreed it was bone white—flashy for a wheelman—but nobody could name the model. Just that it had muscle to it and a loud engine when it tore out onto Vets Highway, squealing in the rain.

Across from the diamond merchant's was a sta-tionery store. Typical Long Island strip mall, a couple of major businesses on opposite corners tacking down the whole line of shops. At one end, farthest from the entrance to the parking lot, was the diamond merchant, at the other a pizza parlor. Chase remembered Lila talking about it. Fratelli's, where they called everybody *paisano* and had wall-paper showing the Colosseum, the Leaning Tower, and gondoliers on the Venice canals.

Flipping through pages in the file, he came to Hopkins's report, written in a quivering hand, re-lating how he and Lila had just finished taking an afternoon's worth of depositions at the court and were driving past the shopping center when they decided to grab a late lunch.

The report was light on human details and heavy on that clear-cut but remote style relating fact after fact.

Chase ran it through his head, heard Lila saying, Son, I need me two slices with extra cheese and if you don't wanna see the unfortunate sight of me growing light-headed and weak in the knees, you won't hog the grating cheese.

Hopkins telling her, Christ, you sure do like pizza. Don't you miss, like, grits?

So they drive in, and Lila spots the bone-white muscle car parked at the curb with its lights on and wipers going. She's instantly aware, maybe even taken back to the night she met Chase. She decides to check it out, drives through the lot, Hopkins going, Hey, I thought you were ready to pass out from hunger?

Chase flipping pages, putting the pieces together.

The three inside men coming out together, still cool, following the plan. Only two o'clock in the afternoon, but it was dark as hell because of the heavy rain. Lots of water glare, cars coming and going with their lights on. It would've been tough to differentiate the police cruiser from the strip mall shoppers. Folks parking to shop at the bakery, single mothers washing clothes at the Laundromat next to the pizza parlor.

Lila pulling up, finally close enough to see the

bagmen rushing to the car, knowing now exactly what was happening. Probably even grinning, thinking, Well it ain't no Bookatee's Antiques & Rustic Curio Emporium heist this time, that's for goddamn certain.

Teeth clenched, eyes snapped shut, Chase going for the cold spot, letting it do its job. The ice running through his brain.

His eyes flashing open.

Hopkins catching on and reaching for the radio. Lila trying to park diagonally across the other car's path, but they were too damn close now. The bagmen piling into their car, both engines shrieking. The rain a brilliant haze in front of the headlights, hard to see anything but halo effect and shadow.

Chase wanting to scream, Don't do it, baby.

Lila throwing it into park, thrusting open the door, and crouching there, getting into position to fire. Hopkins bending low while he shouted into the radio.

The pages tight with tiny scrawls stating what the witnesses saw next. Hopkins unable to confirm because he was ducked down behind the dashboard.

The pro behind the wheel hanging his left arm out the window and firing three times through the driver's door of the cruiser.

Well, look at that.

The driver had killed her.

Not much time left, he knew. The crew would have a fence on hand, but they wouldn't get any cash back from the score for at least a couple of weeks. They'd stick around and hole up somewhere nearby. The fence would probably be one of the mob-run outfits in the diamond district of Manhattan. It was a good guess anyway, something to think about.

Chase played the tape a dozen more times, slowing it down, studying every move, trying to see the things he wasn't supposed to see. Watching the crew move so capably about the place, with no wasted effort, knowing every angle.

So why didn't they take out the camera? Three minutes was tight but they could've spray-painted the lens in five seconds flat. It was pretty much standard operating procedure.

So what was he seeing that he was *supposed* to see? That they wanted everyone to see?

Chase went with his gut.

There was an inside person you were supposed to see acting like anything but an inside person.

That made it either the woman who'd gotten pushed around or the guy who'd gotten slugged in the mouth.

The file had their names and addresses. James Lefferts and Marisa Iverson.

He needed wheels.

Street racing had come back into style, especially in Queens and Brooklyn, and the law was starting to tighten up. Word was that the drivers were now moving out to Jersey to do their dragging, keeping their merchandise in Manhattan and staying clear of the cops who patrolled Ocean Parkway, Grand Central, Kings Highway, the Palisades, and out around LaGuardia. Jersey cops would catch on soon, and then the kids would probably head out to Long Island and haul ass down Route 25a, the Meadowbrook, or the Wantagh.

Chase knew at least a couple of his kids were tooling around the city picking up extra cash doing some weekend racing. They'd asked him the best way to soup their cars for the fast burn, some of them hoping he could set them up with nitrous. He'd never run nitrous himself and thought it was insane to fuck around like that in New York. It was strictly a West Coast way to kill yourself.

Chase took the train into Manhattan and found

the 24-hour parking garage closest to the Holland Tunnel. Security was lax at two A.M. Chase wandered right in past the college kid on duty in the entrance booth who had his face buried in a textbook, snoring so hard that the plastic windows of the little booth rattled.

It took Chase almost two hours of searching the place before he found what he wanted, up on the fourth level.

A 1970 yellow Chevelle. Cowl induction hood, dual exhaust, and fourteen-inch Super Sport wheels. A machine made of muscle.

He got the door open and popped the hood—454 Four Speed with a 360-horsepower engine. It had been cared for, souped pretty nicely but could still use a little fine-tuning. That wouldn't take him long.

The VIN number had been filed down and burned away with an industrial acid. Same with the serial numbers on the engine block. There was no paperwork in the glove compartment. He was boosting a car that had probably already been boosted a half-dozen times since it came off the line.

He slid up to the semaphore arm and didn't even have to run it. He just slowly eased down on the gas and the arm snapped across the Chevelle's grille while the college kid kept dreaming about advanced calculus or subatomic particle theory.

* * *

Chase spent the entire morning adjusting the engine, the brakes, and the suspension, making it all even sweeter. The thief before him had done a damn good job, but now she'd handle even better on the turns.

He switched out the plates and repainted the car a burnished black. While waiting for it to dry he sat in the corner of the garage sucking in the fumes and going back and forth on who might have been the inside person on the ice heist, the man or the woman.

Late afternoon he took the Chevelle out for a test run down Commack Road, ripping it into triple digits and hoping a cop would engage him, but no cruiser ever showed. He pulled it back into the garage and checked a couple of final calibrations. Then, when he'd done all that he could do with the time he had, Chase fell into bed exhausted and dreamed of Lila.

She appeared before him on the bed, twining across his chest the way she usually had during the deep night, and said, "I told you the dead would find a way. You just have to listen to us. So hear me now, love. You gotta let this thing go. I don't want you to follow through with what you're planning. How do you expect me to rest easy knowing what's on your mind? You remember what I say."

He tried to answer her, but when he opened his

mouth all that came out was Walcroft's sound rattling loose from inside him.

He woke in the morning with the pillowcase soaking wet.

He'd been crying like hell in his sleep.

He wasn't hard at all.

The phone rang. It was the principal of the school extending his condolences again. The staff and many of the students had taken up a collection and bought flowers for the funeral, and had Chase noticed them? The remaining fund would be given to the Policemen's Benevolent Association in Lila's name. The principal told him not to worry about returning anytime this semester. An extended leave of absence with pay was in effect. Was there anything that anyone at the school could do? The principal repeated himself and waited for Chase to say something.

Chase said, "I quit," and hung up.

*T*urned out the hero who'd gone up against the crew during the ice heist lived alone in a small two-story house over in Smithtown, the kind of place Chase used to burgle pretty frequently during the early years he ran with Jonah.

It was noon. The time of day when all the kids were at school and the stay-at-home moms and dads and retirees were busy with their soap operas and daytime talk shows, learning how to be better people while slumped on their couches. Nobody ever spotted a cat burglar at noon.

He parked down the block and scoped James Lefferts's house. Lefferts's Taurus was in the driveway, the exhaust still dripping. Looked like he had come home for lunch. Chase waited twenty minutes before he saw Lefferts leave, holding his briefcase tightly

The guy had two black eyes and wore a Band-aid across the bridge of his nose. He was going to have a definite tilt to the left for a couple of months until they broke his nose again and could realign the cartilage. Chase watched Lefferts get in his car and head back to the diamond merchant's.

Chase climbed out and walked through a wooden gate at the side of the house. It led to a fussily kept backyard screened from the neighbors by a high row of hedges. Lefferts lived alone and liked things tidy. Garden gnomes, birdhouses, and little windmills had been planted among the carefully cultivated bushes and flowers edging the perfectly trimmed lawn.

No alarm system. The back door had a dead bolt and the windows were all locked. Took Chase ninety seconds to get inside.

He did a slow and efficient search of the house, going through every closet, drawer, and cabinet. It immediately became apparent that Lefferts was a truly finicky guy. He hung all his shirts on hangers, not just the dress ones but even the V-necks, track suits, and Ts. Kept his sock drawer in perfect order, the whites over here, the blacks over there, his boxers folded and neatly stacked. He recycled and washed out his tuna cans and mayo jars. His electric razor was empty of stubble. All his rolls of masking tape had the first half inch folded over.

The only suspicious items Chase came up with were a box of magazines and videos that bordered on child pornography. Not quite over the line, but man was it close. Some of the stuff was in other languages and came with subtitles. What passed for erotica in Romania would get you strung up in Birmingham. There were also Russian mail-order bride catalogs, featuring mostly pale, seminude chubby girls in ads that read, *My name is Mischa, and I am looking for a successful American businessman who I can love in bed and out. Must own his own home. No children. I prefer no pets but won't mind one small dog or cat. I enjoy oral sex.* These Russkie chicks laid it on the line.

James Lefferts got home at seven. He was putting in the hours, no doubt about his taking the job seriously. Someone like that would probably mouth off at three Colt Pythons when one of his fellow employees got shoved around.

Chase couldn't afford Jimmy getting tough with him now. He needed information fast. He could feel the hours evaporating, the crew getting ready to make their move. They were out there, burning away the downtime until their fence came through with the cash. A couple of them thinking about spending the long green, a couple of others only caring about the juice of the next score. Every string was about the same.

Lefferts walked in and saw Chase in the living room and said, "Who the hell are you?"

Chase punched him in his already broken nose.

Lefferts let out a squawk of agony and dropped like he'd taken an ax to the head.

Blood burst down his chin and across his shirt. He tore at his face with both hands, writhing on the carpet, tears flowing down his cheeks as he flailed and rolled. Chase got some ice cubes out of the freezer, put them in a dish towel, and crushed them against the countertop. When he got back to the living room he saw that Lefferts had vomited all over himself and was only semiconscious.

Pressing the towel to Lefferts's nose induced another cry of pain, but at least it roused him from his stupor. Chase propped Lefferts onto the couch and gave him a minute to wake up.

"Jimmy," Chase said. "Hey."

"Oh Christ, my face—"

"Jimmy, listen to me now. I've got a question to ask you. And I'd appreciate your honesty here. It's very important to me."

"Oh God," Lefferts said, choking on his blood. "I can't breathe, I can't think."

On display in one of the high glass-door cabinets were two bottles of Chardonnay. Chase opened one and poured some into a fancy wineglass.

"Here," he said, "have some of this."

"Is that the Chardonnay?"

"Yeah."

"Did you let it breathe?"

You had to hand it to him. Blood and upchuck aside, he was as finicky as ever. "Just drink it."

Lefferts drew the dish towel away and tried to sip. It made him gag and he started to moan. "I can't taste anything except blood! My nose—"

"You'll be fine. They're going to have to break it again anyway, eventually."

"Lord, no—"

"Now, Jimmy, you listening? Seriously, I need you to pay attention here."

"What? Who *are* you?"

"I want the names of the crew you were working with."

"The what?"

Chase had the box of naughty porn on one of the end tables and pulled out some of the magazines. "I wonder what the feebs will think of this stuff. I wonder what they'll find on your computer when they take it in."

"The who?"

"The FBI. You can delete stuff and rewrite over it on your hard drive and they'll still be able to pick it up. I wonder how many lists your name is on in Czechoslovakia. These child brides that you buy from the former Soviet Union, they know English already or do you have to teach them?"

"You're crazy."

"Do you have any idea who I am, Jimmy?" Chase asked. "If you knew who I was you might understand the lengths I'm willing to go today in order to get the information I want."

"I don't know you and I don't want to know you!"

"You want me to punch you in the nose again, is that it?"

"Fuck no!"

"I'm the husband of the police officer murdered outside your place of business."

Jimmy Lefferts's eyes widened, but it wasn't with fear. It was simply with an even greater confusion. "So what the hell do you want from me? What are you doing? Why are you here?"

"I want to know who killed my wife."

"I don't know anything about that! How would I know anything about *that*?"

Chase got in close, his nose two inches from Jimmy Lefferts's misshapen schnoz, the bloom of blood wafting so pungently, such a painfully human stink. He looked deep and read the man's face. The confusion, the ineffectual anger, the willingness to please, but the uncertainty of not knowing how. Chase finally had to admit that he believed him.

"Okay, Jimmy, I'm leaving now."

"You are?"

"And I can trust you to keep this little conversation between just the two of us, right?"

"Absolutely!"

"I'm sorry about knocking you around, really I am. But if you call the cops or tell anybody else at all about this I'll make sure the feebs come breathing down your back."

"All of my erotica is completely legal! You can't hurt me with that!"

Chase toed through the magazines and thought maybe Jimmy was right. He kneeled, rolled up one of the zines, got it nice and tight and swatted Jimmy Lefferts across his mashed nose. Jimmy screamed and a new stream of blood started running into his mouth.

He waited for Jimmy to focus, pressed a finger to the man's red lips and went, "Then I'll just come back and kill you in your goddamn bed one night."

Her name was Marisa Iverson and she lived only a few miles across town from Jimmy Lefferts. Similar small home but she went in for a pretty high-tech alarm system. It gave Chase some pause while he tried to remember the proper way of tricking it out. Took him a lot longer than he expected. By the time he was finished he was bathed in sweat.

The system hadn't been wired to a security service or the police. Chase wondered about that.

Once inside he made a careful search of the home. A wide living room opened into a dining area, and behind that you had to go through a swinging door to the kitchen. The place was tastefully furnished. She went in for soft blues and paisley, modern lightweight furniture and lots of potpourri and handcrafted wares.

Candles everywhere, a huge CD collection, lots of DVDs held in a large oak bookcase. Mostly guy movies—action blockbusters, shoot-'em-ups, Westerns. The fridge held a lot of beer. A fancy liquor cabinet was filled with a row of half-empty bottles of Jameson, Dewar's, Wild Turkey, and Jack Daniel's. Looked like Marisa Iverson entertained the dudes.

It took him ten minutes to find a Browning 9mm, safety off, buried way at the back of the breakfront behind some fake china and cheap crystal.

Like you're having a holiday dinner with the whole family and somebody says they don't like the soup, so you make like you're going for the gravy bowl and put two in his head.

He pocketed it.

In the bedroom, clipped behind the headboard, he found a .22. He could just see how she'd use it. Lure the mark into bed, take charge and get on top, ride him until he was an incoherent mess, then reach over and yank the little squeaker up, press it to the guy's forehead, pull the trigger. Hardly any blood to clean up. Wouldn't even have to throw out the sheets. A heavy cotton cycle would do it.

He'd have to send some flowers and a get-well card to Jimmy Lefferts. Marisa ran with the crew.

Maybe she didn't trust the string that much. So she kept them lulled and contented with booze and sex and cowboys and Indians. Did she fear a double cross? Did she plan one herself?

He pocketed the .22 as well, walked out onto

the front stoop, and went through the mailbox. Nothing but bills and a real estate flyer claiming home sales in the neighborhood had doubled in the past eighteen months. Chase could believe it.

He continued combing through the house, looking for anything to tie her to the crew that had scored the ice. An address book lay open on her desk. Not many names, most of them local businesses. A dry cleaner's, a carpet steamer service, a local Chinese restaurant. The diamond merchant's office. There was James Lefferts.

Chase figured almost any of the entries could be code and she might be hiding the crew's contact number out in plain sight.

He got on her computer and found a bunch of password-protected files. He tried "diamond," "rock," "ice," and a dozen other words. Driver. Wheelman. Python. Before long a feverish buzz was reaching through his skull. By the time he typed in "Lila" he knew he was starting to uncoil and had to get a grip.

At the back of her bottom desk drawer he found the paperwork for the house. Turned out she was only renting the place and had only been here four months out of a one-year lease. All the blue and paisley and tacky modern furniture belonged to the true owners, cheapo crap left behind for their tenant.

Four months. Just enough time to establish her identity. He doubted she'd been working at the diamond merchant's for any longer than that. He realized then how close he'd come to missing the crew entirely. She wasn't an inside woman at all. She was part of the crew and would be packing up soon to join them.

He stood in her kitchen and checked the dishwasher. A couple of dirty plates, a handful of utensils, one glass. Exactly what you'd expect from a woman living alone. He looked in the fridge again and counted four different brands of bottled beer. He thought the booze was left over from a recent party. She entertained but didn't live with anyone, had nobody dropping by on a nightly basis. Wherever the crew had gone to ground, they weren't near enough to stop by much.

There was no reason for her to continue the ruse now. The longer she hung around the more of a chance the cops would tumble to the fact she was part of the heist. She should've bailed already. Why hadn't she pulled up stakes yet?

Two hours later, at 6:10, the woman who called herself Marisa Iverson walked in the front door clutching her purse and the day's mail. She deactivated and reset the alarm. She put her purse down on the coffee table and tossed the bills in a pile. Then she headed to the bathroom on the first floor. She closed and locked the door. One of those people who followed form even when they were alone in their own houses.

Chase stepped out from the corner of the living

room and went through the purse. Another .22. He figured he'd find more goodies in her car, but he'd let that go for the moment. He took her cell phone and checked the numbers. Maybe she'd slipped up and left him a connection to the crew. He pocketed the phone and the revolver. For a guy who hated guns, he was now packing three of them.

When Marisa stepped out of the bathroom he met her in the hall, said, "Hiya," and clipped her on the chin.

Man she was good.

Even though he'd caught her unaware, she faded back and rolled with the punch. She was lissome as hell and sweet to watch, landing nimbly on the carpet, tucking in, and immediately getting to her feet. He'd hardly even tapped her. He knew it was his own fault. He'd never struck a woman before and had a natural resistance to this kind of situation.

She rubbed the back of her hand against her jaw. No fear in her at all. Completely cool, a total pro, living out on the wire. Maybe she'd been in the bent life since she was a kid, or maybe the crew had picked her up along the way and had taught her well. Chase really wanted to meet this crew.

Marisa Iverson stood and glared at him, her unforgiving mouth tugged into the barest grin. She was maybe thirty, on the pretty side but made down so you wouldn't notice. He saw that she used eyeshadow, rouge, and lipstick to slightly alter the contours of her face. Blond hair drawn back in a tight ponytail, with two twists framing but obscuring her jawline. Big round glasses concealed a lot of details to her features. It was a damn good disguise.

The bone-colored business suit fit her well, but it still somehow looked all wrong on her. Chase just knew it wasn't her real style, and he could see the other person beneath emerging now.

A hard-stepper, she always went at life head-on, and took it as rough as she could because she liked it that way.

"And who might you be?" she asked.

Eyes as dark and lifeless as shale. Alert and sharp as she ran through the current setup, figuring all the different angles, already plotting and scheming.

Chase said, "I might be the Minister of Culture and Communications, but I'm not."

The grin widened. "So sorry to hear that."

"I'll bet."

She had to be wondering if he was just your usual second-story man or a hitter hired by one of the crew to betray the rest. Or if she'd somehow stepped on the mob's toes and now had a syndicate torpedo out here looking for restitution. A lot had to be going through her head, but she revealed nothing, just kept giving that knowing look.

"You don't like to hit girls, do you?" she asked. "That was hardly even a love tap." Saying it like an insult, trying to get under his skin right from the start and shake him up, force him into making a mistake. Soon she'd try to sex him, and then she'd go for one of the guns.

Chase waited. Marisa took off her glasses and tossed them on top of the television. She reached up to her hair and yanked free the scrunchie holding it in place. Shook it out and let it get wild around her shoulders. It had nothing to do with intimacy and everything with baiting the trap.

Clearly she didn't think he was worth being subtle for, and that pissed him off a little.

"So what's next?" she asked. "You plan on spanking me? I hope you are. I know of a much more comfortable place we can do that. I have lots of toys upstairs."

"Let's stay here. I've already seen the accessories you keep around your bed."

It brought a humorless smile to her lips. "Well of course you have."

This one, he thought, this one right here could empty six in my head while making love, and then she'd spit in my blood.

Stepping away very slowly, Marisa eased backward across the living room and forced Chase to follow along. It was a very crafty act and showed she had a lot of patience, moving them toward the table where her purse sat.

"You have any idea why I'm here?" he asked. It wasn't the way to start off, but she'd thrown him already.

"Is that a serious question? I mean, do you actually expect an answer?"

He wanted to take it back and try again. He said, "Listen, I don't care about you or your string or the diamond heist. I just want the driver."

"Oh? Which driver?" She slithered away another inch, inviting him closer.

"He's all I want. The rest of you can walk with the score."

She cocked her head, jutted her bottom lip, and tried to make her eyes soften. As if whatever she said next, *that* would be her being completely, totally, utterly honest. "I have no idea what you're talking about. Really. That's the truth."

Chase sighed.

It was such a forlorn sound, advertising his frustration and sorrow so clearly that it made her let loose with a small yip of laughter.

Marisa Iverson shrugged and held her hands up in front of her, telling him, You expected me to say something else?

It was only an impasse if you didn't have what it took to force your way through. "Your crew was slick but no wheelman carries a gun, much less makes flash moves like firing out the window. Left-handed."

"You smacked Jimmy Lefferts around some last night, didn't you? He was even uglier when he came in to work today."

"It was either you or him."

"Well, I dare say it's him."

"No," Chase said, "it's you, Marisa."

"You're an intense one, honey. Tell me your story. Did some poor girl break your heart?"

"Yes," he said, "you did."

He tagged her hard. Backhanded her so fiercely that she was propelled across the room and over the arm of the couch. She flipped backward and hit the floor, blood already pulsing from her mouth. She turned over laughing and dabbed at her bottom lip with her fingers. She looked up at him.

"I was wrong," she said, "you do like to hit girls. But only sometimes. You're quick on the button."

So he'd told her something about himself. That was inevitable. But she'd let him know something about herself, too.

She only cracked out of turn and broke character when he insulted the driver. There was something there.

She spit blood on the floor, got to her feet, turned, and sprinted for the china closet. Her first instinct wasn't to try for the door but to get the Browning, cap him, keep everything quarantined, under control. She dug behind the crystal and grimaced when she found the weapon gone.

"Got that one too," Chase said. "And I hate guns."

It didn't stop her. She started hurling the plates and glasses at him.

Chase covered up and rushed forward. She kicked out and connected with his shin, then twisted her knee into his groin. It hurt like hell but he fought through the pain. A black shimmer bordered his vision. He slapped her again and she flew into the wall, laughing. She threw herself into his arms and kissed him with her bloody mouth.

"You gonna rape me now, big daddy? Come *on.*"

"The driver," Chase said.

She got her hands on his neck, dug her nails in, and tore them across his throat. He grunted in pain and the gouges dripped blood down his chest. She'd felt the guns in his jacket while pressed against him, and now she had her hand in his pocket, fumbling for the Browning and trying to get her finger on the trigger.

"Christ," he said, and elbowed her in the sternum. She fell to her knees and tried to hammer him in the crotch. He slid backward, got his hands up in front of him like he was in the ring.

He watched her, intrigued and a little sick to his stomach. All his years with Jonah and they'd never worked with a female professional thief. Were they all tough like this? He supposed they'd have to be in order to run with crews that carried Pythons and blew away police officers.

"So, he's your man, eh?" he said. "The driver. He your guy?"

"They're all my guys."

"You must get a lot of chocolate on Valentine's Day."

"You don't have what it takes to roll with me," she told him.

"We can find out if you really want to push the point."

"Oh," she said, chin already swelling and growing black with bruises, gums purple with blood. "I do. I certainly do, baby." Turning action into foreplay. "Your hand is shaking."

"All I want is the getaway man."

"Hold your arms out, maybe he'll fall through the ceiling right into them."

Chase was tough, but he didn't know if he could do whatever it took. Not even now. Not with Lila still alive in his mind, imaging her eyes filled with disappointment and love for him. Jesus, what the hell was he going to do?

"Marisa, I'm kind of appealing to you here, okay? Really. Neither one of us wants to go down this road."

"You are such a cunt," she said. "You're easy. You want to know how easy. Watch." She came at him again, and when he tried to hold her off, she went at him with her teeth. She turned her head and chewed into his wrist.

He smacked her and then backhanded her, rocking her off her feet. It was a couple of mean shots but not nearly enough to make her stop giggling. Her eyes had told him that she didn't think he could do the things he would have to do. She kicked out at him and he hit her again. She struck the floor with a snarl and lay there with her shoulders trembling, spitting out looping ropes of blood. He watched her, knowing she was laughing at him.

"Like I said, you're easy."

"Marisa, don't make me do this."

"I'm not making you do anything, baby. But it's all right, we'll be done here soon anyway, and then you'll get yours."

Here it was, finally. He was meeting the worst part of himself. He thought of the men who hurt women. The driver blasting Lila. The animals out there that he'd always despised. The bastard murdering his mother.

Chase raised his fist and punched Marisa in the face, the sound of bone cracking bone making his belly twist. She had guts and she stuck to the rule that you never gave up your crew. She'd never break and he felt an odd respect for her, mixed with all the disgust and hate. How far could he go?

Mouthing Lila's name, he slugged Marisa Iverson again. She barely rocked back on her feet. Her eyes were beginning to close up. She wobbled and dropped, and then shot to her feet again, moving for her purse. He let her go. When she found that the .22 was gone she hurled the purse at him. It bounced off his chest. She turned to face him, still grinning, she'd be grinning in his dreams, he knew, for the rest of his life.

"The driver."

"You'll get nothing out of me, baby," she said.

The Jonah in his head said, Shoot her in the stomach.

Sneering, Marisa came at him once more and pummeled him twice in the chest. She knew how to throw a punch the right way, trying to stop his heart. Then she drove an elbow in his ribs and he almost went down. It filled her with joy and adrenaline. No wonder she and the driver had paired up. She was a lunatic too.

She ran in and tried to bite him in the throat. He slapped her two, three, four times bringing loud grunts and weird laughter from her. She fell to the carpet, tried to stand once more but couldn't. The surge of crazed energy was fading.

She started panting and moaning a little singsong that reminded him of the preacher overtaken by the power of tongues at his wedding.

Finally she managed to stand, weaving a bit.

"You think I can't take a few love taps?" she said. She spit at him, her blood landing on his shoes. "I've been getting worse than this since I was seven years old. You can't hurt me. You can't do anything to hurt me."

Jesus Christ, she might be right.

He was teeming with sweat. He wanted to moan or roar. He would fucking beg her if he thought it could work.

She was better than him, much harder than him. As icy and tough as they came. But he couldn't shake the thought, even now. Why hadn't she pulled out of town yet? What was keeping her here?

And then he knew why she hadn't run yet.

He'd botched it.

If only he'd waited and watched a few more days, he could've caught them all. He'd messed up, hadn't been thinking clearly.

The crew planned on scoring the diamond merchant again.

"You're going to have to kill me now, you know," she told him. He wasn't sure that she could even see him anymore. "You don't have any choice. The minute you leave I'll just call my boys and they'll scatter. Or worse for you, they'll hunt you down."

"They won't have to." He found an unused pad and pen next to the phone and wrote his address down. "They can come find me whenever they like."

"You're insane," she said, the smile gone at last. "You can't just walk away."

"Sure I can."

"I won't let you."

"Tell them I'll be waiting."

"Cunt."

After all of this she still managed to launch herself at him, trying to scratch out his eyes. He caught her in midair easily, held her closely for a moment, and then laid her onto the couch. Her adrenaline finally gave out and she slumped back across the cushions, out cold.

Shadows lengthened across them both. He stared down at her unconscious form as the room grew darker, the sun starting to set. His hands were sticky with her spit and blood. He didn't move. He didn't know when he would be able to move again but he knew he couldn't move now.

She was protecting the one who had squeezed off three shots into his wife.

He should take her kneecaps out.

He should put two in her eyes.

The guns were heavy in Chase's jacket. He tried to will himself to accept and become a part of their exacting pitiless nature, even while Lila said loudly within him, Oh sweetness, what've you done?

*C*hase found himself in the dining room drinking a beer. He finished the bottle and left it in the sink. On the couch, Marisa Iverson gurgled, hissed, and snorted, having a hard time breathing with her face so swollen. He made for the door and another thought hit him.

Carpet steamer service.

Marisa Iverson had only been planning to stick around for a few months at most. Establish an identity at the diamond merchant's, make the move on the video cameras, stay long enough for the heat to dwindle, and then she and the crew would score the merchant again.

So why the hell would she feel the need to clean the carpets? How dirty could they get that someone in the bent life would care enough to pay to have them cleaned and keep the number on hand?

Chase ran upstairs and got her address book, made a note of the steamer service address and phone number.

Maybe this was her one mistake.

She'd be unconscious for another hour at least. He had that long to see if he could track the crew on his own.

It took him fifteen minutes to get there. The address was real. He drove by it and found an industrial park. She knew the area and had gotten just a touch too clever trying to cover every detail in order to make her sham life seem authentic. She was organized and compulsive. She couldn't put a number down in the book without an address too. She couldn't put an address down if it wasn't an actual place.

The number would belong to a cell phone. It would be untraceable, and it would be ditched a minute after he called.

He had only one shot at this, and he had to make it count.

*There was probably a code they stuck to when con-*tacting each other. Two rings, hang up, three rings, hang up, some kind of shit like that. A lot more discriminating than on Jonah's circuit.

Chase called the number. After it rang twenty times, he disconnected and tried again.

They weren't a twitchy bunch but there would be rules to follow. No matter what though, even if they figured the cops were on the line, they'd eventually have to answer. It was Marisa's phone, they'd need to find out what happened to her and see how badly their action was blown.

After another twenty, a dead-calm voice said, "Yes."

"Are you the getaway man?" Chase asked.

Silence.

Let him roll it around for a while, get the questions burning, but without being able to ask any of them. Give nothing.

Chase said, "Are you the driver? All I want is the driver. I left a message with Marisa Iverson. I'll leave it with you too. I don't care about your knockoffs or what happened inside the ice merchant's. I just want the driver. Don't tell me he was your regular guy. A maniac like that firing out a car window on a heist is a wild dog. The cop killing has got to have put a lot of heat on your ass. Give him to me and the rest of you can walk."

"No."

"Then I'll take you all down. You the driver?"

Silence.

"If not, pass the word on."

Chase broke the connection and threw the phone out the car window. He got onto the Long Island Expressway heading east and put the hammer down until he hit 110. The world blurred around him but not enough. Traffic parted before him like flesh opening before the intent of a knife.

He shut his eyes and drifted, hearing Jonah telling him he'd fouled up again, leaving the girl alive and warning the crew. When Chase opened his eyes again and checked the rearview he had three cruisers trying to box him in, the sirens and lights suddenly surrounding him. He smiled his first real smile in weeks, squeezed out 135 from the engine and watched them fade behind him as he jockeyed around family SUVs. Before any more backup showed he took the next exit off, parked behind a firehouse until all the sirens dissipated in the distance, and stole a

fresh pair of plates. He took back roads toward
home. Every time he looked in the rearview and
saw his own eyes he got a minor jolt. He kept
thinking someone else was in the backseat, scruti-
nizing him.

He called Murphy in Fort Wayne and found out the man was dead—heart failure, six hours on the table, ten weeks in a coma before finally giving it up—but the elder son, Georgie, had taken over the crime line while the younger son ran the used-car lots. Georgie knew who Chase was and said, "You still a grease monkey?"

More stupid-ass code. The old men had been using it since 1958. They still said "dropped a dime" and never knew how much a phone call cost. If the feds were listening, how hard would it be for them to fucking reverse the numbers?

Chase said, "Georgie, listen closely. Forget the double-talk. Tell me where Jonah is. I need to see him."

PART
IV

Georgie gave him a phone number, in reverse. The guy was going to carry tradition right to the end.

Turned out Jonah's current home base wasn't that far away, only an hour upstate in White Plains. Chase couldn't figure the attraction in White Plains unless Jonah was using it as a headquarters just to be close to Connecticut, maybe the Indian rez casino. It wasn't Jonah's usual type of score, all those people and the serious security, but Chase had no idea what kind of heists his grandfather was putting together now.

He called the Deuce and asked a lot more questions, got a few answers. He needed to scrape together whatever facts or rumors he could find out about Jonah's dealings over the last decade. Deucie said he'd get back to him after he talked to a few other guys, but the information was going to cost and yes, he took credit cards. Chase ran off his Visa number.

A day and a half went by before Deucie phoned back. He'd talked to a lot of people who still liked Jonah and a lot more who didn't. There was even more bad blood out there now. He told Chase what he'd wanted to know and said, "If you're getting back into the life I think I've got someone who could use you."

"No thanks."

"He's a don's son, has a pretty solid crew. Good money and he likes guys who can handle cars and trucks."

That meant the mob was back to doing a lot of big-rig hijacking. Send out crews to work the highways, the syndicate bosses robbing from each other. It was low-class, the families must be having a lot of troubles with each other lately.

Chase told him, "I'll think about it."

"Hey," Deucie said. "I was sorry to hear about your wife. Really, I got to tell you. I mean, if it was my wife, it would be a blessing if she got taken out, you know? The way she's an anchor around my neck, what with the leather shoes and the Gucci purses and the jewelry, and always with the Mexican pool boys. I turn around, there's another fucking Mexican unclogging the filter, she wears these guys out. Me, I let it slide, I don't know why, maybe one day I'll hire a torpedo to bury her in the Pine Barrens with all the goddamn shoes and purses. But you, I remember what you did when she got hurt couple years back. You, I can tell, you actually loved—"

Chase hung up.

*   *   *

He dreamed of his father and called out his name. Michael. Chase was nearly as old now as his dad had been when he'd offed himself. It made them brothers of a sort, a part of the same fraternity of pain. He wanted to hear his father's voice, and more than that, he wanted his father to hear his. A powerful urge swept through him to offer whatever guidance he had to his father. Maybe it would be enough to save him, even now, fifteen years too late. Keep him from taking the boat out in a storm and capsizing this time.

The past drew at him in a way it never had before. His childhood before Jonah seemed to be swarming up, loud and prevalent, trying to yank him backward. He kept watching his father in the snow, cheek pressed to the frozen marble tombstone, wanting to be dead.

Chase knew he was dreaming because his old man suddenly entered the room. It was too dark to see but he knew the body language, the expression of sorrow in every movement. So this was his dad after his mother's murder. He called out the man's name again and told him to leave. He barked like a wounded dog in his sleep because his father was sitting on the end of the bed, weeping.

Chase phoned the number that Georgie had given him and got a genderless voice mail. He left his home address, set up the meet for three days from now, and named a busy family restaurant near the LIE where two parkways intersected. It would offer Jonah four directions to run in case he smelled a trap. Chase couldn't think of anywhere safer that his grandfather might feel secure enough to meet with him after all this time. Jonah's first thought would be that Chase was still in the life, had been arrested, and was now setting him up on a plea-bargain.

Chase wondered what else he should say—*Hey, why the hell didn't you at least send a wedding card?*—but nothing sounded right. *How's it been going, you doing okay?* Besides, Jonah wouldn't want to hear any sappy shit. He'd either show or he wouldn't.

He'd set the meet for noon, but knew Jonah would leave him sitting alone at the site, checking him out from afar to make sure it wasn't a sting, making certain no cops had followed. Jonah wasn't about to come out from cover here. Chase parked at the restaurant, climbed out of a beat-to-shit '72 Plymouth Gold Duster he'd stolen that morning, sat on the hood, stretched back over the windshield and took in the sun, thinking of Lila.

Forty-five minutes later he got up, slid into the car, and started back toward his house. Jonah would've checked out Chase's story and made sure he knew where Chase lived. The old man would have the route back all mapped out with a good ambush site already chosen.

Jonah never followed anyone else's rules. He always made sure he got the drop.

It was all right. Chase knew exactly where Jonah would make his play. There was a wide exit down the parkway that opened up onto a service road near a community college, bordered by wooded acreage. Jonah would cut him off, shove him onto the shoulder, and grab him right there. Chase had planned it this way from the start.

Behind him, way back on his left but beginning to speed up now, a white van jockeyed forward. Chase slowed down right as the exit lane came into view, thinking, Here it comes, here it is.

He wondered if his grandfather would hit him. He thought the old man was going to get at least a couple of free slugs in. Jonah didn't feel things like other people did, but somewhere inside him he must've still experienced a small sting of betrayal about how they'd parted.

The van tore out from behind, speeded up alongside the Duster, and crashed into the left front quarter panel, forcing Chase over the curb and into the pine trees. It was a skillfully executed move, pinning the car in the brush and giving him nowhere to run.

His jaws snapped together painfully, and his head rang. He tugged the wheel hard to the left and tried to bump back, but the Duster was already a buckling rust bucket and the crumpled metal blew the left front tire. He stabbed the gas and allowed himself to smash into a tree. The seat belt tore against his chest and he swallowed down a shout. There was an insane uproar of noise as the front end buckled and the windshield caved.

Pretending to be dazed, Chase slumped over the steering wheel, glass in his hair. He quietly un-buckled himself because his ribs hurt like hell and he didn't want Jonah to haul him against the belt a few times before thumbing the button. The car door swung open and rough hands yanked him from the seat.

Chase offered no resistance. He went down on his back in the grass. The van door slid aside and he was yanked to his feet. Chase tightened the muscles in his belly, waiting for the old man's fist. He raised his chin and there was his grandfather.

At sixty-five Jonah remained hard and looked mostly the same as when Chase had last seen him ten years earlier. For a guy who should be on social security he was still ready to take on a brigade. His back straight, arms corded, every ridge cut to perfect definition. Same steely eyes.

There were some subtle differences. His face had eroded further, almost imperceptibly, like desert stone after ages of high wind. The seams went deeper, the mileage and wear a bit more apparent. The black hair on his arms had gone mostly white so the sprawl of muddied prison tats appeared much clearer.

Chase could finally see them for what they were now. An angel on the left forearm and a devil on the right, both in midflight with drawn flaming swords.

And names.

Under the angel: *Sandra*, *Mary*, and *Michael*.

Jonah's mother, his wife and his son, Chase's father.

Under the devil, peering through a pitchfork: *Joshua*. Jonah's father.

And beneath that, not a tattoo but a scar that had gotten infected and was still mottled white and pink.

Chase.

Huh, look at that. Chase had to wonder, was it a comment made in flesh about disloyalty? Is that why his name went on the evil arm? These cons, they sure liked their fucking Biblical imagery.

His grandfather said, "Some getaway man."

Jonah hurtled a fist into Chase's gut, threw two jabs into his nose, got blood flowing, and then tossed him in the back of the van.

Still pretty nimble, Jonah hopped in, quickly frisked Chase, and then kneeled on his chest.

A woman was driving. That was certainly something new. She turned back and gave Chase a quick once-over with distinct dark eyes. Woman, girl, she was maybe twenty but you'd never mistake her for a kid. Even through his tears he could see she was on top of the action, in control, her gaze knowing. If she was anything like Marisa Iverson he was already in deep shit.

No hesitation. She hit the gas and the van tires spun, throwing gravel.

Jonah said nothing and neither did Chase. The knee in his sternum hurt like hell but he'd known it would have to go down like this. And it didn't hurt nearly as bad as that day Lila had kicked his ass on the garage mat.

Now they were going to drive around for a while until Jonah was sure they weren't being followed. Then they'd finally take Chase back to their local hideaway.

He checked his grandfather's left hand. Jonah was palming the .22.

The van hummed along. The girl was pretty good behind the wheel. Lying on the floor, Chase could feel the vibrations and shifts as she moved from lane to lane, driving easily and with a deft edge. From this weird angle he could see her in fine detail but upside down in the driver's seat. She wore tight blue jeans that hung back off her hips, a black thong pulled way up, and a leather vest tight enough to nearly squeeze her tits out the sides. Putting it out there just daring someone to make a run at her. Flat muscular midriff on display, pierced belly button with a gold hoop. A small tattoo of a grinning dolphin on her stomach, poised as if it was leaping through the hoop.

Chase couldn't figure her, and it took a minute for things to lock into place. Jonah must've felt like he'd slowed down a half step over the years and needed to make up for it. Dressed like that, the girl was there for distraction. Even a pro's eyes would linger on her for an extra second, and that would help even things up.

Looking down at him she smiled sweetly. "I'm Angie."

Chase said nothing, waiting for Jonah to feel safe.

She took the next exit and headed south toward the bay. In ten minutes Chase could smell the ocean. He decided they were holed up in the Islip area, somewhere around the ferry launch. Jonah must've gotten a room in one of the shabby motels just north of Montauk Highway. A once ritzy area that was now a bunch of cluttered dive neighborhoods. Former mansions broken down into low-income boardinghouses, outpatient re-hab centers, and homes for the mentally chal-lenged. A lot of seedy old-man bars down by the train tracks. It would be a good drop point if Jonah decided not to trust Chase. He'd get a few drinks into Chase and pop him with the .22, make it look like a suicide in the midst of despair after wrecking his car. Or just dump him in front of a Babylon local. The plan had holes in it but all the best plans did. It kept the cops stumbling.

The pressure on Chase's chest eased as Jonah stood and Angie turned off the road, slowed, slipped into a spot at the curb, and threw it into park. The clanging bells of a railroad crossing erupted, followed by the scream of a whistle. A train was pulling in. Chase checked his watch—1:28. They were in downtown Bay Shore.

Angie looked back at Chase and said, "Come on, let's get inside where it's comfortable. No troubles, right? Wipe your bloody nose with the bottom of your shirt."

Jonah gestured at the van door with his chin and Chase got off the floor, wiped his nose with his shirt, slid the door open, and stepped out. They were at a motel/bar called the Wagon Wheel. Tucked behind the station, the place looked like every other flophouse where the lifelong drunks and prostitutes shacked at the very end of their games. It was also the sort of spot commonly used as a meeting ground for thieves putting a string together and scheming a heist. Civilians never saw anything or remembered anything, and even if they did, they made unreliable witnesses for the cops. Chase had spent a lot of time in similar environments.

His grandfather put a firm hand between Chase's shoulder blades, steering him to a room around back. Angie unlocked the door and said, "Welcome to our humble abode. Feel free to put your feet on the furniture."

Chase sat on a ratty couch with no life left in the springs, backed against the far wall so he was the farthest person from the door. It would be how Jonah wanted it. Angie sat at the other end of the couch and Jonah took a ladder-back chair facing straight on. Usually it would've worked the other way around, you always sat as deep in the room as possible in case somebody kicked in the door. But when you were watching somebody, like his grandfather was watching him now, this was the only way to work it.

For the moment it was Jonah's play. Chase waited. He was losing patience fast but figured he could hold on until—well, until he couldn't any longer.

"Let's have a drink," Angie said.

A bottle of scotch and some glasses were on the coffee table. She poured three fingers into each glass and pushed one in front of Chase. He threw back half of it in one pull.

The girl sipped, smiling, trying to put out a breezy atmosphere. She kicked off her shoes and put her bare feet against Chase's leg. Her toenails were painted torch red, the same as her fingernails.

The only reason he knew the name of the polish was because Lila had once tried it and said, "Any woman ever approaches you with these nails who isn't your wife, even if you spot her in the first pew of church Sunday morning, she's a whore or practicing to be one."

Jonah wasn't good at dealing with people and Chase could see that Angie was the front player. It probably made her feel slick and accomplished, but all it meant was that if trouble ever marched in, she'd take the first bullet.

She moved her foot toward his lap and he wondered if she was just the playful sort who enjoyed prompting men or if she was hard like Jonah and this was some new challenge devised to test Chase's sincerity. Whatever it was, now was the time for Chase to quit backing up and make a move. Jonah would be waiting for it. They wouldn't be able to get the ball rolling until the tension broke.

"Isn't this nice?" she asked. "So how long's it been since you two old friends have—"

Chase flipped her legs aside and kicked the coffee table toward his grandfather. The old man was a little slower than he had been, but that didn't matter much. He was primed and had something to prove. He dropped his left shoulder to bat aside the wobbly old table. It wasn't going to hurt him. The .22 came up in his right hand and he started to lean forward. Chase did too.

Chase was fast. Maybe faster now than ever.

He could've snatched the gun away from Jonah like he'd taken Lila's that first night. Chase's head was crowded with doubts and misgivings about a lot of shit, but he had no question about that. He could've driven his fist into his grandfather's belly or whipped low and bird-dogged him, tackling him across the lower legs and possibly shattering his knees.

Chase was certain he could've done any of those things, but none of them would get Jonah to help him. And it would wind up killing one of them. So he forced himself to hesitate.

It was painful doing nothing while you waited for the rest of the world to catch up.

The bottle of scotch hit the floor and bounced twice, landing right side up without spilling a drop. One of the glasses struck the radiator and shattered, the others rolled across the stained carpet.

Angie reached beneath a cushion and started to clamber off the couch, moving up behind Chase. She took tiny nips of air between her teeth. She'd cleaned her weapon recently and used too much gun oil.

Without expression, Jonah pressed the .22 to Chase's forehead.

Maybe a full two seconds later Angie shoved a Bernadelli subcompact .25 into the mass of nerves under Chase's left ear. It filled his head with electrical colors and his teeth started to sing, but he didn't resist.

The three of them stood there like that waiting for the next moment to pass.

Staring into the old man's icy-gray eyes, Chase asked, "Are you going to help me or what?"

Without lowering the gun, Jonah said, "Talk."

Chase told his story as succinctly as he could, hardly mentioning Lila at all. The truth and depth of her, the perpetual excitement and warmth she pressed to his heart, it would be lost in the speaking. He knew Jonah wouldn't understand revenge like this, where the act was more important than the payday.

Paring down the details of the last ten years, it only took Chase twenty minutes to lay out his whole life up to the moment that Lila was killed. It left him stunned and a little angry to realize it.

It took another twenty minutes to cover the rest of it because Jonah would need to know every detail Chase had found out about Marisa Iverson and her crew. He left nothing out. When he mentioned the part where he'd worked her over with body shots, Angie let out a wild laugh and said, "Chip off the old boy's block, eh? Your technique must be genetic."

By the time Chase was done his hair was crawling with sweat, but at least that part of it was over.

The next local came through, the whistle like a bayonet slicing through the slim, water-damaged motel walls. Now that he could relax he heard noises wafting in from the other rooms. The noise of a whiny john haggling over the price, trying to get a cut-rate deal on some kind of deviant action. The whore held steady because it wasn't part of her regular policy. Working girls of her caliber didn't go in for that kind of kink. Sixty extra, and he had to pick up another fifth of gin. A door slammed. A figure rushed by the window, heading for the bar to purchase a bottle under the table, which would cost him an extra ten over retail. This guy really wanted to do his nasty thing.

"How do you know I wasn't in on it?" Jonah asked. "The ice score."

Chase sat up. "At the time you were on the run after pulling a score with Matteo and Lorelli in Aspen. You tried to clear out two side-by-side mansions in a gated community, using a couple of the private security guards as inside men. One got scared at the eleventh hour and called the cops, hoping to be a hero. When the job went sour you nearly got pinched. It's rough making a getaway from mountain towns. Both guards went down. Lorelli was aced. You left him there. A couple of his buddies apparently have issues with that. Now you're in White Plains. Casing the Connecticut rez casino?"

"You did a good job of checking me out. You still have connections besides Georgie Murphy."

"A few. Some of them helped because they respect you. Some because they hate you."

"No," his grandfather said, "it's because you paid."

"Sure, but it doesn't change what they feel."

Jonah kept those eyes like polished river stone on Chase, seeing if he could crack him with the stare. "Maybe you'll give me those names later on."

"No."

Jonah nodded and turned away, thinking about it all so far, maybe realizing that he wasn't as on top of the game as he thought he was.

The nasty guy came back, slammed his room door again, and got busy drinking gin and doing his thing. Chase gave a little more attention to Angie, who was sitting there making her silent assessments.

She had a natural provocativeness but wasn't what you would call beautiful. Black hair, dark features, he thought she must be Spanish. Nose a little too long, her lips not quite matching up. Small, thin scars were almost hidden in the seams around her eyes. Some stitching indents at the corners of her mouth. She'd been mishandled and had had some plastic surgery along the way to put her looks back where they belonged.

He wondered how much weight her word carried with Jonah. Was she a full partner or just a piece of some string who'd come along with Jonah for the fun of it? Was she in on the rez deal, if there was one?

He supposed it didn't really matter. She was merely someone else he couldn't trust. The .25 wasn't on view and he couldn't decide if she'd jammed it back under the cushion or had it tucked somewhere on her person. If she had it on her, under those skintight clothes, he couldn't figure out where it might be.

Angie spotted him looking and mistook his intention. She let out a little smile and held his gaze, attempting to appear demure. It didn't work and she seemed to know it but was determined to give it a go anyhow. Maybe practicing on him, gauging his reaction. When she didn't see what she wanted to see she glanced away, took an unbroken glass off the floor, filled it, and offered it to him. He threw it back. She poured another and sat there sipping it.

"Letting the woman go was stupid," Jonah said. "She was the one advantage you had and you gave it up. Phoning them was even worse. Now they know you're on to them."

"I want them to know," Chase said.

"That's not the way to do it."

"It's the way I'm doing it. Are you going to help me or not?"

"Depends. I still don't know what you want."

"I want the driver."

Only three o'clock, but the traffic was thick, bottle-
necking them among a fleet of eighteen-wheelers
as they hit some construction on Sunrise Highway.
The road crews stood around holding jackham-
mers and shovels but not using them, and the left
lane's asphalt lay peeled open. The van didn't
have the best suspension and the stop-and-go jerk-
ing started to bounce the whiskey inside Chase. He
shouldn't have drank. He wasn't used to it and the
sourness made him think of the stink always drifting off Joe-Boo Brinks.

He looked over at Jonah and the Jonah inside
his mind said, He wants to ace you, but he's waiting. He'll grab the score, put one in your head,
and leave you at the scene.

Chase didn't need to give Angie directions to
his house. She already knew the way, which was
pretty good for someone who hadn't had more

than a couple of days to set up the snatch and memorize the roads. He thought more and more that she wasn't just along for the ride. Nobody had mentioned her being in on the Aspen heist, but Chase wondered if she'd been there with Jonah and Lorelli, and if she'd been the driver who'd gotten them out of the tight mountain town.

She caught his eye in the rearview. He still couldn't figure her but decided to think the worst for now.

They came down his street toward the house. He got out, keyed in the garage door code, and said, "Pull all the way in."

He'd taken down the heavy bag so there was room for the van beside the Chevelle. Angie threw it into park They got out and Jonah stared at the black Chevelle.

"You still got something to shred the road," he said.

"It's new," Chase told him.

He opened the door to the house and led them inside.

"You don't keep it locked," Angie noted. "You've got no burglar alarm. You'd think a cop and a thief would know better."

Chase said nothing. It bothered him having Jonah here, in the home he and Lila had made, even though this wasn't the same home anymore without her. It meant less and less to him every day. But he could sense his grandfather already scoping the silverware, checking around for loose cash, plotting to walk off with something. The loss of property didn't matter, Chase had already decided to get rid of it all and sell the house. He didn't regret giving everything up, but he didn't want the old man to steal any of it.

Angie went through the fridge, grabbed fixings for sandwiches, and said, "We're hungry."

"Most of it's probably stale."

"That doesn't bother us. Anything to drink?"

"Only what's in there."

"There's nothing in there. Guess we'll finish the scotch."

Plural again. Angie spoke like she was half of an old married couple, and he wondered if he was hearing it right or reading into it. He could imagine them lovers. Jonah always went in for the young stuff. But he'd never heard a woman talk about the old man like a husband before. Jonah's silence lent itself to the idea that he felt the same way about her. Chase regarded them without any interest as they both ate, throwing back the whiskey, Jonah eating and drinking the way he did everything else. With no wasted action, no sign of enthusiasm, utterly emotionless.

When he'd finished he asked, "So what do you need me for?"

"You already know that," Chase said.

"Yeah, I do. You don't want to get your hands dirty."

"I'll get them dirty, I just want you there to help me do what needs to be done."

"Don't talk in euphemisms, it only muddles the situation."

"I'm going to kill the driver," Chase told him. "The others too, if they get in my way. That clear enough?"

"You got the stomach for that?" Jonah asked.

"You either believe me or you don't."

"You said you nabbed the store's security videos of the heist from the cops?"

"Yes."

"Let me see them."

While Jonah viewed the tapes in the den, Angie wandered the house touching stuff, picking up framed photos and putting them down again. Grabbing up knickknacks, the vases and candles, looking at the paintings and prints. Chase followed behind, watchful. She said, "You like clutter. Or your wife did."

Chase had never thought about it before. He said, "You need to fill a home."

"I wouldn't know. Never had much of one. My mother croaked when I was nine. Uterine cancer. You ever see what that does to a woman? It makes her horrified that she *is* a woman. Knowing the part of her that *is* woman is what's killing her. She died with this look of confusion and terror on her face. My father was a Cuban boozer who loved the

Miami club scene and thought he was a gigolo for the pasty-white divorcees. If he was lucky they'd let him drive their Porsches home. They'd tip him like the pool boy. We lived in a two-room apartment. He'd spend eight hundred bucks on a pair of shoes, but wouldn't have money to feed my sister and me. He got drunk at a club, hit on some drug dealer's woman and got snuffed in the men's room when I was eleven. He died with his head in the toilet. My aunt took us in. Altogether with her kids there were fourteen of us in her house. I started turning tricks as soon as my tits came in. Hooked up with a third-rate crew in St. Pete's Beach a couple of years later. At first I was just there for laughs, but soon I was planning some easy jobs. We wound up moving around a lot for a while. Then I got on a string with your grandfather and stayed with him after the boost."

"When was that?"

"Three years ago."

"You couldn't have been sixteen yet."

"I wasn't."

She turned away just when she got to the part Chase wanted to hear about. "When did you go to the cosmetic surgeon?"

It made her lips stiffen. "I don't like to talk about that."

"Scars look pretty fresh."

You never mention such things to a woman, and he knew it. But he needed more info and hoped she had enough vanity left to let something slip.

Angie just breezed out a giggle. "You bastard."

Yeah, she was definitely hard, with that same sharpness and ability to take pain that Marisa Iverson had. He wondered if she'd picked it up on her own or if Jonah had helped her find it along the way.

She grabbed up a photo of Lila and Chase sitting beneath a wild maple with a blur of children rushing by in the background. "She was pretty."

"Yes."

"Looks like a picnic."

"Down the road from my in-laws' house. They had a lot of family."

"The way you say that, I can tell you never considered yourself a part of it."

"I did my best."

Brushing a fingertip over the edges of the photo, tapping with that red nail where the river jutted just into frame. "Where was this taken?"

"In Mississippi."

That surprised her. "You spent time down south?"

"Seven years or so."

"Usually when someone's there for that long they pick up a hint of accent. You don't have any."

"I've been back in New York for a while."

"That's not the answer. You've never had an accent of any kind, have you. Not even a New York one."

Chase shrugged. He'd been a lot of places and talked how he talked.

"You really going to kill this crew?"

"If I have to. If I can. I only want one of them."

"I don't see it in you. I've known guys who could put down their own mothers, but you—" Her eyes searched his face, looking for every character flaw, each weakness and desperate intent. The lips turned up in a soft kind of sneer, the scars dimpling back into view. "I don't think you could put down a dog."

"Depends on the dog."

"I think the old man will have to get it done for you."

"We'll see."

He'd found where she'd stashed the Bernadelli. There was a small extra pocket right at the bend of her left hip. Easy to reach and draw from, and the subcompact showed almost no bulge as she moved. The pocket fit a regular seam in her jeans. She knew how to sew too.

Chase's hand flashed out and he snatched the .25 from her.

"Hey!" she said.

Only nine ounces, he couldn't believe how light it was. Less than a toy weighed, no wonder these people liked to pull them so often and keep them so close. There was a sense of power without the burden of potential murder.

He said, "You use too much oil."

"I get overzealous. I like things clean."

"No use hiding it so well if someone can sniff it out on you. You walk into a score posing as a lady just doing her banking or shopping and one of those retired cops turned security guards will know you're carrying."

"I'll remember to dab on more perfume. Now give me my sweet little cap gun back. You don't want me throwing a tantrum."

He handed her the pistol and watched her slip it back into the secret pocket, where it vanished once more. "That's a clever hideaway."

"And you're a naughty boy, dipping your hand in there like that. If you want something, all you need do is ask."

"I'd like to know how you hooked up with Jonah."

Her eyes deadened for an moment and then brightened again almost instantly. "It's simple enough. I was with somebody else and now I'm with him."

"You don't sound too happy about it."

"Sometimes I am, sometimes I'm not."

"You can always move on."

"No, I can't."

He decided to drop that. "What happened to the somebody else?"

"He left."

"On a gurney or by his own free will?"

"He made a mistake and died for it."

"Who snuffed him?" Chase asked.

The smile again, the near-invisible scars adding some mystery and strength to her features, and something else he couldn't name but which made the muscles in his back tighten. "Who do you think?"

Jonah poured the last of the scotch in a glass and took a deep bite. He didn't look the least bit interested in helping Chase. "What's in it for me?"

At least he put it on the line, first thing. Chase had expected him to say that. He'd assumed from the beginning that he'd have to offer money up front on top of a possible score. At the time, the idea of it hadn't offended him, but now that he was staring into his grandfather's face, he found that it did. It stung knowing that the man would never do anything except for a payday, not even for someone whose name was tattooed into his flesh.

And Lila had once asked Chase if Jonah had ever really loved him.

"I'm selling my house," Chase said. "The price of real estate is still shooting up on the island. I should clear at least a hundred grand, maybe more."

"And I get it all?"

"Sure."

"You're not even going to try to talk me down, see if I'll do it for less?"

"You'll cost whatever you cost."

"And when do I get it?"

"The house isn't on the market yet. A few months, I guess."

"And I trust that you're good for it?"

"I'm good for it. Whether you trust me or not is up to you."

Jonah showed nothing. "Let me think about it."

"No," Chase said. "I need an answer now. If you shake off then I go it alone."

"How much time do you figure you've got left?"

"Almost none. The fence has had over a week to start moving the ice. He'll have sold some of it by now, and he'll have a small amount of cash to hand over to the crew. The woman, Marisa Iverson, didn't cut and run when she should've. I think they're going to score the same diamond merchant again."

"So they're close."

"Yes."

"Maybe closer than you think."

Chase frowned and said, "What does that mean?"

"It means you never should've given them your address." Jonah stepped back into the living room and clicked on the video. "If they were smart they would've hit you immediately. When did you brace the woman?"

"Four days ago."

"So they're good but not that good." He paused the video where Marisa Iverson was getting shoved. "She'd have to hide out after you worked on her. She could call in sick for a couple of days, stay away from her house. But if they want to go through with scoring the merchant a second time, they'll want her back in play. If they're worried about you fouling the deal, they'll have to move on you first." His gaze roved across the TV screen. "She's got to be fucking the manager of the shop."

"What makes you say that?"

"Because it makes sense." Jonah rewound, hit play, and pointed out the manager. A puffy guy in his mid-fifties with a bad toupee who stood around looking mildly irritated the entire time the heist was going down. "She's the insider for the crew and he's the inside man for her. Feeding her information on when the diamonds are due, what the safe combination is, all that. He's probably married to a cow and nailing this piece on the sly. Look at him. He only gets upset when the crew pretends to rough her up. He thinks he's in love with her. She's driven him out of his head."

Chase hadn't considered the possibility of a second inside person. He hadn't been able to get into the head of a lonely, middle-aged white-collar guy.

He thought about Marisa Iverson moving in his

arms, forcing her blood-smeared mouth against his. The manager, yeah, he'd enjoy that taste.

"I see it now," Chase said.

Jonah leaned over and tapped the TV screen. "You can tell. Everything in his life is an annoyance except for when he's in bed with her. She takes him to a whole new place, and he's desperate for that feeling now. He never wants to go back to what he was before. The straight citizens, most of them are so bored they want to snuff themselves." Chase looked at the manager being annoyed, wanting out, barely able to contain himself with Marisa in the same room. "The cops will work on him, but right now he thinks he'll go to the pen before he gives her up. Never underestimate the desperation of a man who has everything."

The manager would be a liability now. She'd have to get back into play and deal with him. "He's going to want to run with her."

"They'll cap him this time, on their way out, before he spills to the police. If the crew wants that second score they've got to go in fast. But they can't move quick because of you. They know you're watching, and since you were stupid enough to tell them where you lived, and they were stupid enough to wait, that means they're watching you."

His grandfather was right, Chase had been stupid. He'd been so caught up in his own grief and anger that he figured they might want to come at him the same way he wanted to go at them. Head to head. It hadn't occurred to him that they might be more subtle and monitor him for days.

"You think they're somewhere nearby this minute?" he asked.

"Sure," Jonah said. "They should've punched your ticket already but they think you're on to them, baiting a trap. They believe you're a pro because you got this close. By now they've aced one of your neighbors and have somebody installed."

A crew that would murder a civilian in his own living room, just to keep an eye on somebody. Maybe the driver wasn't the only wild dog. Marisa Iverson was at least a little crazy, going through what she had for the sake of the driver, who'd popped a cop. Chase had been thinking too positively. He wasn't going to get the driver without taking them all down.

He glanced at Jonah, who was staring back at him.

"You didn't think anybody else might get hurt in this fight of yours?" his grandfather asked.

Chase said nothing.

They moved to the front window together and peered through the blinds. Jonah pointed across the street on the diagonal. "Who lives there?"

Sarah Corvis and her kids. They'd sent over a roast after Lila's funeral. "A middle-aged woman, has a teenage son and daughter."

"Too many to take out and keep quiet." Jonah pointed to the house opposite it. "There?"

The Wagner family. The children had brought over a card. "Husband, wife, three children grade-school age."

"No." Now, pointing down the block the other way, again diagonally from Chase's house. "And there?"

Mrs. Nicholson and Freddy. Freddy would sometimes walk to the very bottom of the lawn and watch Chase tune the car, but he'd never come any closer than that. "Elderly lady, seventy, seventy-five. Has a mentally handicapped son who's maybe fifty. They're shut-ins, live on government checks, have their groceries delivered. They have lots of cats."

"Call her."

Chase got out the phone book and dialed the number. He let it ring ten times and hung up. He swallowed thickly, thinking of the poor woman, in her kitchen, Freddy in the bedroom, the cats going hungry. "No answer."

"They're dead."

He didn't waver or tremble, but inside he fell in a heap and the hatred bloomed further, for the crew and himself, and he was screaming.

The volume inside his skull was turned way up. He had trouble hearing his grandfather.

"When it gets dark we'll go over there for a visit," Jonah was saying. "Pack up your shit because we're leaving here. We'll get another place up near the diamond merchant."

He held out his arm and Angie immediately slid next to him. He toyed with her hair and she plucked at his fingers, as if they'd practiced the action many times before, like a dance neither one of them enjoyed anymore.

Jonah told Chase, "Stand watch for a few hours, we're tired from the trip. You think you can handle it?"

Lila had liked Mrs. Nicholson and Freddy. She used to go over there and bring pies. She'd made the effort to be generous and sociable. Chase never had. He'd be out in the garage working the speed bag and Lila would come back from across the street with her breath smelling like peach cobbler and say, "No reason under God why such lovely people as them have got to be alone in the world. Living in a houseful of cat piss. That Freddy, he admires you." After the funeral, Freddy had come a little farther up the driveway and waved.

Even Freddy had made the effort, and now he and his mother were dead because of what Chase had set in motion. The Jonah inside his head said, You didn't think anybody else might get hurt in this fight of yours?

He'd be saying it forever.

Still putting Chase to the test, Jonah wanted to see how far he could push. He walked to the master bedroom and said, "We'll take this one."

"No," Chase told him.

"You're alone, you can take the smaller bed in the guest room."

"No."

Thinking now, So maybe this is where I get to shove that popgun .22 up his ass.

He looked at his grandfather and his grandfather looked at him, and they both stayed that way for a while until Angie pressed a hand tenderly to Jonah's face and made him turn aside, then tugged him down the short hall to the guest room.

Jonah, who didn't feel things like a regular man did, but somehow still acted like someone stung by an ungrateful child. Chase turned back to the window and stared at Mrs. Nicholson's house, imagining the scene.

The crew wouldn't let the driver go along because he was a wild card and might try to pop Chase without first checking him out thoroughly. So one of the others would be sent in, someone who liked to work quietly, maybe with a knife. He'd park up the road from Chase's house, checking out his house and everybody on the block. Watch the kids play, the men cutting their lawns, the women heading off to work or shopping. See Mrs. Nicholson limp out onto her front stoop to get the mail or pay the paperboy. Contemplate Freddy standing out on the cement driveway doing nothing.

So he'd knock on the old lady's door and say he was selling Bibles, keep a conversation going while he scanned her place, making sure she lived only with the retarded guy, except for all the cats. The

stink of the cat piss would make his nose run. He'd
look out her front window at Chase's house and
wonder what was going on in there, why Chase
had fuckin' invited the crew to come crush him.
There had to be some kind of setup.

The old lady asking him, Aren't you going to
show me the Bibles?

What Bibles?

The gold-inlaid fine end-paper illustrated and
annotated text Bibles that you're selling.

Maybe knifing her right then. Or, not wanting
to get any blood on himself, just strangling her,
garotting her. It didn't take much to snap the neck
of an eighty-year-old woman with osteoporosis
and light bone density.

Freddy letting out a perplexed and terrified
shriek. Or maybe not, maybe just standing there
unsure of what just happened. Going, Ma? Ma?

Standing there going, Mama? While the knife
appeared. While it slid into his belly and the great
overwhelming pain engulfed him, but still not great
enough to drown out his fear for his mother. Ma?

Falling to his knees, then on his face, the cats
scattering.

The killer calling his crew and using their little
code, two rings, hang up, three rings, hang up.
Whatever. Telling the boss, the schemer behind it
all, I'm in.

Watching the house across the street, seeing
Chase come and go. Now a van pulling up with an
old man and a hot chippie with him, sliding into

the garage. Watching the blinds part a little bit in the living room over there now, somebody staring back out at him.

Chase went for the cold spot and let it ice him down, the burning fury that threatened to consume his thoughts slowly being quelled until he could think again.

He stood watch, staring at the house for four hours. He heard Jonah and Angie in the guest room going at it. Maybe not so tired from the trip, after all.

Chase remembered being thirteen, and Jonah holding the mostly empty pint of Dewar's and introducing him to the cute and less-cute girls named Lou. His grandfather had stolen the one Chase wanted to be with simply because he could. It had nothing to do with sex and everything to do with power, which reminded him of Marisa Iverson and why Chase had called Jonah in the first place.

They were two of a kind. He'd been right. He needed Jonah.

Chase stood at his front window staring into the evening as it became night, wanting to kill someone.

*B*y the time Jonah was ready, Chase had a bag packed with a few changes of clothes and some personal items. There was nothing else he wanted from the house. The bag was out in the trunk of the Chevelle in the garage. He'd brought in many of Lila's guns and laid them on the kitchen table.

"In case you want something to carry."

"Yours?" Jonah asked.

There were things he would talk about and things he wouldn't. Chase didn't want to say anything about Lila to Jonah. The very act of discussing her with his grandfather seemed disrespectful to her memory.

So he said, "Yes."

"Don't need them right now. Got a .38 I like. But pack them up and bring them along. We might have use for them later."

Chase still had Marisa Iverson's 9mm and two

.22s, all three of which he'd cleaned. He felt more comfortable with them than he did with any of Lila's weapons. It was a complicated emotion that he couldn't quite untangle.

But he knew that thinking about Lila would make him soft, even if only while holding her pistol. His concentration would fail, even as it was failing now, his mind wanting to take him back to her, to hear her laughter, think about her smile. He had to hold on.

Angie walked out of the guest room and picked up Lila's twelve-gauge shotgun. She checked the load and racked it. "I'll be able to hold the fort with this."

"We won't be far," Jonah said. "We'll cut through the backyard, circle around the block, come up behind the house."

Mrs. Nicholson's place was dark except for one dim light in the living room.

The sun had only been down a few minutes, but Jonah didn't want to wait for fear the crew might come by and make a hit before he and Chase could get over there. They went out the back door, hopped the fence, and worked their way through neighboring yards, circling in a wide arc.

There was a sense of time moving very quickly now. The understanding that it was running out, or had already run out, and they could do nothing but wait for whatever was so nearby to strike. There was no averting it, no deflecting it.

Chase was very quiet but still louder than Jonah, who moved silently and kept to the shadows like he owned them. They spotted and avoided motion-detector lamps, property with dogs, a couple of loud households where rowdy cadres watched a late baseball game. Everybody was losing money on the Mets.

They got to Mrs. Nicholson's backyard and eased through an overgrown hedge. Chase put a foot on the lawn and felt something brush his ankle. The cats were loose. Seven or eight of them, slinking about, pooling in the gray patches of light bleeding through the clouds. Their eyes glowed a fiery amber, and the curves of their fangs were outlined in blue detail. They mewled and meowed. Whoever was inside had tossed them out and they were aggravated about it, maybe starved.

Jonah whispered, "Make sure none of them follow us inside."

Chase and Jonah moved to the back door, which opened into the kitchen. Jonah let him take point, of course. He'd expected that too. He had a very clear image of getting gut-shot and lying there while Jonah ran away and ransacked Chase's house, stealing Lila's candlestick holders.

The thought of it made his shoulders tighten. Jonah noticed and put a hand on his back, pushing forward because he thought Chase had frozen with fear. The old man really never had known him at all.

Drawing his tools out of his jacket, Chase got to

work. It took fifteen seconds to pop the door. He inched it open and squirted oil onto the hinges so there wouldn't be any squeaking.

A sharp crew but maybe not sharp enough. The guy should've blocked the door with something— a chair, a beer bottle, a stack of glasses. Anything to warn him that somebody was coming in, but he hadn't taken the precaution.

So, either an oversight or a trap.

Chase crept in, his grandfather at his heel.

Mrs. Nicholson and Freddy were seated at the kitchen table. Side by side. Their heads almost touching.

At least Chase figured it was them. Two body-sized shapes wrapped in garbage bags and cocooned with duct tape. The roll was still on the counter. The bodies didn't stink all that much, considering. The cat piss smell overpowered it.

Chase thought, Because of me, because of my mistakes.

He tasted Marisa Iverson and didn't know what it meant until he realized he'd bitten through his tongue and his mouth was full of blood.

The fire began to burn again but he fought off a wave of guilt and forced himself to stay focused. He pulled the 9mm, hating the feel of it in his hand but adoring its intention.

The guy was napping at the front window, sitting in a worn love seat with an MP3 player in his hand and the tinny sound of music coming from his earplugs. He'd been here a day or two and the boredom had made him sloppy.

He was slim, a little younger than Chase, with a pretty-boy roguishness and his hair moussed all to hell. Probably took him forty-five minutes every morning to affect that nonchalant hipster messiness. Dressed down in a wife-beater T-shirt and stained jeans. Young girls would've found him beautiful.

Chase didn't get a pro vibe off this guy. Something was wrong.

He smelled setup but couldn't see any kind of trap. He quickly walked up and cracked the fucker across the head with the butt of the 9mm. The guy's eyes shot open and then quickly closed again as he tumbled to the floor. The solid thunk of metal on bone was so satisfying that Chase had to restrain himself to keep from doing it again and smashing the guy's skull in.

Jonah had drawn his favored .38 and was searching through the small house. He returned and gave a headshake. Nobody else in the place.

First thing Jonah did was rifle the guy's wallet and pull all the cash. Looked like three or four hundred bucks. Jonah pocketed it and checked the driver's license. "It's a fake. Shitty work too. Looks like it was glued together in a half hour. First time stopped at a traffic light he'd be busted. Name on it is Timmy Rosso. He can't be a pro, sleeping on the job. They killed the old lady and her son and then suckered him into taking this fall."

"Is he carrying a phone?"

Jonah found the guy's cell and handed it to Chase. Only one number programmed in. Terrific, he thought. Now we have to go through this shit again.

Chase walked away and Jonah said, "Where are you going?"

You couldn't do much but you had to do something. Chase went to the back door and opened it, letting in the cats. There were empty food and water bowls in the corner of the kitchen. He found the cat food under the sink, filled the bowls, poured water, and watched the hungry cats tearing in. He turned and stared at the figures of the dead old woman and her retarded son wrapped in their own garbage bags. Lila was in his head saying, Sweetness, you gone far enough for me, I'm proud of you. Now it's time to stop. And don't let that granddaddy of yours touch the good silverware.

Jonah stared at him like he'd gone insane, which was fine. Chase found a vase full of dead flowers, filled it at the sink, walked back into the living room, and tossed it in Timmy Rosso's face, dried stems and all.

As the guy came awake Chase looked at Rosso, pointed the 9mm in his face, and asked, "Hey, any chance you're the driver?"

The look Jonah gave him said, What the fuck kind of question is that? He knows you want the driver. Even if it is him, he won't admit to it.

That's because Jonah didn't understand that wheelmen had their own thing going. They wanted to be known. It set them apart like the old-time juggers, the safecrackers. Or the demolition men, who were the only ones willing to touch nitro. They had special skills, talents that made them distinct from the rest of the string. It made them a little vain.

If it was him, he'd say it.

"No," Rosso told him, dead flower petals in his dripping hair. Blood pulsed across his forehead and threaded into his eyes. "I don't do that." There was a whine and some real fear in his voice. "And I didn't kill those two in the kitchen either."

"I didn't think so," Chase said. "Do you know who they were?"

"No, I never saw them. They were already . . . covered when I got here."

"So who snuffed them?"

"I . . . I can't say."

"I think you can."

"No, really, listen to me—"

Chase held up a hand and cut him off. Rosso wasn't one of the string. The guy was holding back out of fear, not loyalty or professionalism. They'd hired him especially for this part of the job, to watch and report, and then go down.

"All I want is the driver."

"The driver of what?" Rosso said. "I don't know what you're talking about."

Was this another desperate man who had everything but still needed Marisa Iverson?

"What do you know?" Chase asked, sounding tired even to himself. "Come on, tell me your story."

Trying to hold out, Rosso struggled with himself and ran all kinds of scenarios through his mind. His eyes danced and darted. Chase could tell the kid was thinking about throwing himself out the front window, tucking and rolling, doing some kind of ninja shit. He started to pant and flex a little. Gearing himself up to launch at Chase, fight him for the gun, shoot his way out.

"This is why you always tie them up before you throw water in their faces," Jonah said.

Chase nodded.

But the fact was that Rosso remained too dazed from the blow to the head to think clearly enough about how weak he was. If he tried to get up, he'd fall over on his ass. Chase waited for him to try.

Rosso tried and flopped out of the chair and landed among the cats. You'd think they'd been rehearsing this gag for a while, the way the cats just watched him fall and then slunk against him.

Chase picked the guy up and threw him in the chair again.

"I'm going to call you Timmy, okay?"

"It's not my—"

"I know it's not your real name. I don't care about your real name. But I need to call you something, right? So, Timmy, tell me about the crew who set you up in this house with these dead bodies."

Rosso began to cry.

It wasn't something Chase had been expecting and it made him break out in a sweat. Rosso continued sobbing. He really was only a kid, in way over his head. Chase figured Marisa had fucked and scammed him too. Given him the bad fake ID to make him feel like a part of her lifestyle. She would've promised to take care of him.

The guy tried to talk through his blubbering but Chase couldn't understand the words. Chase went, "Shhh, shhh, it's okay."

Finally Rosso calmed down, tried again, and managed to form coherent sentences while he sniffled. "I don't know any crew...I just know Mary and Gus."

"Tell me about them."

"You already know Gus. That's what this is all about."

"Sure," Chase said, "but pretend I don't know Gus. Just tell me about him and Mary. How you met them, all that, okay?"

"Well, she's...she's...my girl. He's...her husband. You know this!"

Jonah drew out a knife from a sheath at the small of his back. A two-inch blade, which was more than enough if you knew what you were doing. He moved in on Rosso very quickly. His face, as always, showing nothing. Rosso's eyes grew wide and he parted his lips to shout. Jonah covered the kid's mouth with his left hand, almost gently holding it there in an oddly loving gesture, then stabbed the blade down into the thick meat of Rosso's leg.

The kid dropped forward with a muted shriek and Jonah held him there while Rosso wailed beneath Jonah's thick, callused palm. Tears again spurted from the kid's eyes and he sucked air loudly through his nose.

Jonah mimicked Chase and said, "Shhh, shhh, it's okay. I just want you to stay focused and tell the truth, okay? Tell the truth and you'll get to go home soon. All right?"

It took a couple minutes but eventually Rosso managed to nod.

The leg wasn't bleeding much. The knife had

only gone in a half inch and the wound had sealed around it. Jonah moved his hand from Rosso's lips and saw that the kid had vomited a little. Jonah left the knife in Rosso's leg and wiped his hand on one of Mrs. Nicholson's cats.

"You . . . stabbed me."

"Keep talking. Now. Come on."

"She's married to Gus," Rosso said, panting, "but he doesn't take care of her the way she needs, all right? I met them at the Plead the Fifth in Smithtown, on 25a. It's a hole-in-the-wall joint, I'm a bartender there. They just moved here from Sacramento, and he can't find a real job. He's done time and he's drifted in and out of drugs. You know all this! Please, my leg. Get me a bandage."

He made as if to grab the blade and Jonah said, "Don't you touch it."

Chase told him, "In a minute, Timmy, we'll call a doctor. Come on, keep going."

"She started coming in alone and, well . . . she wants to leave him. He hits her, she had bruises on her face. He beats her and makes her do things. With his friends. With you! She doesn't love him anymore."

"She loves you now."

"Yes."

"Go on."

"What do you want? What do you want from me?"

"So what did she tell you about the people in this house? And about me?"

"About your deal with Gus."

"What deal, Timmy?"

"Don't call me Timmy. About how these two were your partners, and you double-crossed and killed them because you've got a big shipment of drugs in your house and you're going to sell them to Colombians and make at least a hundred thousand dollars. Afterward, when you were sleeping, I was going to steal the cash. And then you and Gus will probably go back to Cleveland where him and Mary grew up, and me and Mary can go anyplace in the world with the money. Maybe go to Italy and buy a villa. She wants to visit Italy."

Jonah said, "Nobody can be this stupid."

Chase was awed by the clever manipulation. Take a dumb, immature, mostly honest kid, make him think he was in love, give him an awful task like sitting in a house with two corpses, and so long as he thought it was for the right reasons, saving his woman from a brute of a husband, he'd do it with no hesitation at all. She'd even worked in the bruises Chase had given her and used them against the kid as well. The fact that none of it made any sense only added to the beauty of it. Rosso was a romantic, and he was more than willing to believe the fairy tale. Details only would've confused him.

He'd been in this house for two days and had never really looked at the pictures on the walls. Photos of Freddy, of Mrs. Nicholson as a young girl, as an old lady, all the cats. Shelves and shelves

full of framed photos of the cats. Crochet and knitting magazines on the coffee table. Balls of yarn
and knitting needles in a wicker basket on the end
of the couch. And yet when Chase looked in
Rosso's terrified eyes he saw the kid really believed
all the idiotic shit he was saying.

Chase asked, "So what makes you think Gus is
from Cleveland if they said they were from
Sacramento?"

"That's because of the guy with the scar. Please,
my leg. It really hurts!"

"Forget your leg. Tell me about this guy with a
scar."

"One night Gus came in alone for a couple of
beers. I hate him. I hate him so much I thought of
putting ground glass in his beer. It's a sin what he
does to her. But I can't do anything until after the
deal goes down. So he was sitting there and . . . and
a guy with a scar going across his forehead comes
in and sits next to him. They pretended they
didn't know each other but I could tell. It's in the
body language. They made a big show of shaking
hands and introducing themselves, but I knew."
Holding his chin up, trying to eke out the last of
his courage, Rosso did a pretty good job of it. "I'm
not stupid, you know."

"I know," Chase said. "Tell me about Cleveland."

"The guy was whispering. He said imagine if
they'd hung around in Cleveland like their fathers. They'd both have had heart attacks and her-
nias by now. Meanwhile, this guy, his forehead all

disfigured like that, looks like he went through a windshield."

Maybe the driver. Why a public meet? Because they were both getting antsy holed up for so long, waiting for the fence to get back to them?

"You did good, Timmy." Chase held up the cell. "Now, what's the stupid phone code you're using?"

"No code, Mary just picks up."

"What have you been telling her about me?"

"That you're always in the garage tuning the car. And that your connection showed up this afternoon."

"What did she say to that?"

"She said she couldn't wait to get the money. She couldn't wait to be with me. We're in love. Gus—"

"Yeah, I know, Gus is a piece of shit. When was the last time you spoke to her?"

"Around then, when he showed up with you in the van."

"When are you supposed to contact her again?"

"About twenty minutes ago."

Chase hit REDIAL and the phone rang once and immediately went to voice mail. Marisa Iverson's voice came on the line and said, "You're too late. I know who you are now. Sorry about the wife. See you on the road."

Chase disconnected and said, "Shit. It could be too late already. They might've scored the merchant this afternoon. Put on the television."

Jonah switched on the set, and it was all over the news. The diamond merchant had been robbed for a second time in less than two weeks. The manager was dead, shot right before the thieves left. James Lefferts's nose was swaddled in bandages but he seemed comfortable in front of the cameras this time.

Lila's photo appeared behind the cute newscaster and they brought the whole thing up again.

"They're out," Chase said. "All of this was a diversion."

"You're the one who gave her the edge," Jonah said. "She was a step ahead. I'd like to meet this woman."

"No, you wouldn't," Chase told him.

They had Marisa Iverson's face but they didn't really have *her face*. They'd never track her from the employee photo or security tapes they had. She'd pitch the glasses and let her hair down, wipe off all the overdone makeup and let the strength and confidence cut loose again. No one would take her for the same woman.

Timmy Rosso stared at the TV but still didn't make any connection. He said, "Look, I don't want the money anymore. I just want to leave. Me and Mary, we'll go, right now, tonight. You'll never see either of us again."

Jonah walked over to Rosso and tugged the blade out of his leg. A small spurt of blood came along with it, a dollop arcing onto the carpet, just missing the cats. The kid screamed and this time

Jonah let him. Rosso fell out of the chair and gripped his leg, thrashing.

The old man started to raise his .38 and Chase gripped his wrist.

Jonah was still incredibly strong. Chase could only keep hold of him because Jonah allowed it. His grandfather stared hard into his eyes and said quietly, "We have to kill him."

"No."

"He was watching us."

"He was watching me. And so what? He's got nothing."

"He can describe me to the cops."

"And tell them what? That he was keeping my house under surveillance while he sat here with two dead bodies wrapped up in garbage bags? Nothing he could say to them will make any sense at all."

"It's still trouble we don't need."

"He was a sucker. He doesn't have to die for that."

"That's how everybody dies."

There was nothing else to say to that. Either the old man would make his move and Chase would be able to stop him, or he wouldn't. If nothing else, his grandfather broke the complicated world down into a much simpler form. Every moment brought you right up to the edge. You could either win against him and live, or lose and die. Sometimes it was nice not having so many options to choose from.

Jonah watched Rosso another minute and finally turned away. "All right, but let's wipe this place and leave now, before he stirs any more shit."

Chase had planned on it anyway. He'd touched the back door, the cat food, the water bowl, what else? He looked around, seeing the photos again, thinking of Freddy staring at him in the garage, wondering how in the hell anyone could kill an old lady and a retarded man who never stopped smiling.

Had he touched the kitchen table? Had he brushed against the garbage bags? He couldn't take any chances, he had to clean it all. The cats looked at him. He took a step toward the kitchen and caught a blur of motion from the corner of his eye.

Rosso said, "Oh God, no—" as Jonah took hold of the kid's hair and eased his head back to expose the throat.

Chase moved and opened his mouth but nothing came out except Walcroft's noise.

Fast, his hands always so fast, but now, for some reason, he was far too slow as he reached out and Jonah jabbed the guy called Timmy Rosso once under the left ear, severing the carotid.

Then the old man cleaned the blade on the dying kid's pant leg, two smooth strokes back and forth as Rosso's face contorted into a look of profound amazement, and his hand started to come up, reaching with some urgency for Jonah's hand the way a helpless grandson might reach for him across a short distance of enduring darkness.

PART
V

*Three A.M., with only a glimmer of moonlight maneu-*vering between the slats of the blinds, Chase stood at the window staring at the house across the street thinking about the three corpses inside with all the hungry cats. How long before that became the stuff of urban legend and this town got put on the map by PETA's newsletter? Images twisted at the back of his skull and he let out a soft grunt. He thought about dropping an anonymous tip, but then the cops would canvass the neighborhood and show up at his door asking if he'd seen anything suspicious, and that would just spook the shit out of Jonah.

Lila, he thought, I'm seriously fucking up here.

He leaned back against the dining-room table. They couldn't go to the motel now. There was still a chance the crew might make a try for him. They should take the loot and pull a fade, but maybe he'd made it personal enough for them to come take a poke. He hoped so.

He thought maybe the driver would show up at around midnight, gunning his engine in the driveway, flashing his high beams, and they could finish this thing the right way. Race against each other out in the streets, see who could stay on the road the longest. It was the only real shot he had left.

Which meant he had no shot at all. His mind was wandering again. The rage squeezed up and tried to take him over. He crossed his arms and tightened his hold on himself. He had no cool right now. He had no cold.

He'd played his hand poorly. He'd waited too long. He'd focused on the wrong things. The woman never should've been let go. He'd burned the bridge.

A stakeout at the merchant's would've been dangerous but it might've worked. If the cops hadn't spotted him. If the crew hadn't spotted him.

He hadn't thought it through clearly enough. He'd brought Jonah in too late. He shouldn't have brought him in at all.

His grandfather had grumbled a little about not being able to score the crew now, but he fully expected his hundred grand from the sale of the house. It was a big payday for doing nothing. The old man could head back to White Plains with his girl and pull whatever score he had cooking there and just collect the cash when the time came. Chase would hand it over, thinking, Who cares?

The door to the guest room opened. The only light on in the house was the forty-watt bulb over the sink. In the dark, Angie padded to the refrigerator and started making another sandwich. She was naked. She stood there silhouetted, grabbing the last slice of cheese, a few wilted leaves of lettuce, a final squeeze of mustard. She ate quickly, gulping her food.

Her body was muscular and shapely, her ass streamlined. Chase wondered if the old man had sent her out here to test him. But no matter how he turned it over he couldn't figure out what the test could possibly be for.

Or was Jonah just concerned with showing off? Saying, Look at what keeps me warm at night.

The gold hoop in her pierced navel gleamed. The grinning dolphin tattoo, poised as if leaping through the ring, was winking. He hadn't caught that before. He also hadn't noticed the light stretch marks. She'd had at least one kid. So where was it? With her aunt back in Florida? Did she hand it over to an adoption agency without even looking to see if it was a boy or a girl?

Angie knew Chase was behind her. She didn't mind. She didn't turn. He sensed her knowing attitude, the confidence in her stance even while she swallowed down her last bite and made for the water jug. As she bent, a soft ripple worked from her upper back to her shoulder to her arm. Her ass wriggled the slightest bit. She stood and started to sip, her breasts silhouetted in the dim fridge light, her throat working. With the back of her hand she wiped her mouth, then sighed and shook her hair out. She held the jug between her breasts and her nipples hardened dramatically. She turned.

Her eyes found him in the dark.

They burned with understanding. They stripped him down layer by layer. Chase could feel himself being peeled back and opened up until he was as naked as she was. He wondered if she would go deeper and get to his very center.

"You know," she said, "he talks a lot about you."

"Yeah?"

"Even before he got word from you. He used to go on and on."

Chase stepped into the kitchen. "You're kidding."

"I don't do kidding."

No, of course she didn't. "So what did he say?"

"Oh, about the scores you pulled together when you weren't even a teenager yet. How good you were slipping into houses and, later on, behind the wheel. How all the strings respected you, even though you were only a kid. He says those few years when you were together were his happiest time in his whole bent life. He's also sorry he didn't come to your wedding."

Chase looked at her. Angie was lying but he didn't know why. Jonah might've talked about his past, told her some of the stories and given her the facts, but there wouldn't have been any sentimentality. He wasn't capable of it.

Who the fuck did she think she was kidding? Was she trying to spare Chase's feelings or to make him feel tighter with Jonah in order to lull him?

Angie wasn't grinning but the dolphin was. The damn thing distracted him more than her bikini wax. She took another sip of water and a dribble escaped down her chin. He knew he was supposed to lick it off. She tried to put a smile in her eyes, but he read only a hint of fear and impatience.

Then he knew she was trying to humanize the old man. Make him seem less hard, even a touch loving. And weak. Not invulnerable. She'd overplayed her hand but he didn't want her to realize it. Angie was ready for the next thing and had to make some kind of a move in order to get out. Now that the score hadn't gone down, she was ready to cut free of Jonah.

And she wanted Chase to kill him.

It made him realize how imposing Jonah still was. Here was a woman who laid him, saw him go naked into the shower, slept beside him. Who could press her .25 to his head at any time she liked if only she could overcome her terror that he might wake up at that exact moment. And she still couldn't do it. Which is what had saved her so far.

"He loves you, you know," she told him.

"Sure," Chase said.

"In his own way. In the only way he knows how, being who he is. What he is."

"Yeah," he said, sounding like an idiot even to himself, which in this case was good. Maybe it would get her to underestimate him.

"You're the only one he loves. Everyone else he destroys. More than you know."

Where was she leading him? She was trying to drop subtle hints now so that later she would really have him hooked. What wasn't he picking up on?

Chase tried to see it, wondering if he ever did pop Jonah, and Angie was right there beside him, how long would it take her before she put the Bernadelli in his ear and vented his brainpan? Would he make even ten seconds? No, five tops.

She said, "Don't feel too upset about what happened over there."

"What?"

"I can see it's eating you up. He only did what you invited him here to do, right? What you couldn't do yourself. It's what you expected, isn't it? What you were hoping for?"

He nodded because there was nothing else to do.

He had known. He must've known that when Jonah had turned away from Rosso and said, *All right, but let's wipe this place*, the old man was lying. The old man had never conceded on anything, had never said all right. Chase hadn't believed him about anything else, so how could he have trusted him about that?

Chase hadn't. He'd known when Jonah had

drawn the knife that there was no way the kid would ever be let go, no matter how dumb he was.

Chase was fast. He should've been able to reach his grandfather. But he hadn't even tried.

"I can make you feel better," she said, and eased toward him, her tits bouncing lightly, her body expectant. She tried smiling again and this time made it. She wet her lips. "Even if it's only for a little while, I can make you feel good again."

"No," he told her, "you really can't."

Lila sat with his mother at the kitchen table. There were bagels and cream cheese. Steam rose from two coffee cups and wavered in the air.

It wasn't the kitchen in this house. The table setting was familiar but he couldn't place it. Maybe they were in Mississippi, or maybe this was where his mother was murdered. He couldn't remember.

They were talking quietly together, in deep conversation. There was an air of importance to it all. Lila's tone grew more urgent. He kept waiting for her voice to rise and call out for him, but she continued in the same hushed manner. It bothered the hell out of him, knowing they were sharing secrets. Was there anything more awful than your mother and wife trading info about you? Christ. There was that whole sisterhood thing. They'd talk about shit that would send guys screaming out of the room.

His mother responded with a strange calm, her expression almost smug. The two of them going back and forth, being a little petty about it now since they were both pulling faces. Chase, struggling to move nearer, was unable to do so. He tried to speak but couldn't hear himself.

Both women looked up with a start. They stared at him with real worry. His mother's features quickly shifted into a frown, and Lila gazed at him with loving concern.

He'd made another mistake. What had he done wrong?

The dead will find a way. They'll make you listen.

He tried to speak again and this time heard himself say, "All right, I'm listening."

In weak and unrecognizable voices, they began to speak

Angie stood at the foot of the bed, gripping the toe of his shoe. He'd slept in his clothes again.

"You were moaning," she said. "You woke us."

Chase cleared his throat and said, "Sorry."

Behind her, Jonah stood wearing nothing but briefs, looking well laid and rested, holding his .38. There wasn't an inch of sag on him, his muscles were still large and cut. His chest was thatched with thick white hair. His numerous scars were even more marbled. A couple of old bullet wounds, some knife slashes, a lot of beatings. You looked at his body and you couldn't figure out how anybody had survived all that. He glanced at Chase but said nothing. He silently receded and half a minute later there was the sound of the shower.

"What were you dreaming about?" Angie asked.

Chase sat up and scrubbed his face with his hands. "I don't remember," he told her, wishing it was the truth.

He finally noticed she was dressed in Lila's clothes. A rose silk blouse he'd bought her for their first Christmas in Mississippi together, and black leggings that Lila only tried on once and said made her ass look too big. They hadn't. They didn't make Angie's ass look too big either. They held tight and really drew the eye, which seemed to be the reason she'd chosen them. The .25 must be in the waistband at the small of her back.

It meant she'd gone through the drawers while he was sleeping. He shouldn't have been so out of it, but the lack of sleep had finally caught up with him, and the nightmares were getting worse.

He looked at her, trying not to show anything.

"I hope you don't mind," Angie said. "I wear the same size your wife did."

"So I see."

"She had good taste. Not exactly mine, but very nice anyway. We had to leave most of my stuff back in Aspen when the last score went bad, and I haven't had a chance to do any shopping." She checked herself in the mirror. "Does it bother you?"

Chase fought to smile. He was glad he couldn't see the result. "Not at all. You look wonderful in them."

"Thank you for that. All women like a passing compliment, even me, and I never put too much stock in them."

"Why not?"

"Too many guys use them just to fuck you. Fuck your cunt or fuck you over. But they're still nice to hear."

He didn't quite get that one, but let it slide. He got a change of clothes and used the three-quarter bath to take a quick shower. When he got out, the old man was just finishing up in the other bathroom. Jonah had spent a hell of a long time in there. He hadn't put the fan on and the steam burst into the corridor. Maybe he'd needed to loosen up, his muscles bothering him after all the sneaking around through the neighbors' yards last night.

After Jonah got dressed, Chase took them out for breakfast. He drove by the Nicholson house without glancing over at it. Jonah was looking nowhere and everywhere, and Chase knew his grandfather must be wondering if he'd soon drop an anonymous tip. If Chase would be able to take the idea of a house full of bodies right across the street.

The dream had helped him on that point. Chase already had his own house full of bodies, he didn't need to sweat another one.

The Chevelle wanted to roar and he wanted to with it, really let it rip up the street. But he tamped the need down, holding on to it. There'd be another time. He knew right then, there was still one last chance. He held on to it the way he gripped the steering whccl. With dead-white knuckles.

At the diner, while they ate, Angie slid a slice of raisin-bread toast almost between her teeth and left it perched while she asked, "So what are you going to do now? Go back to teaching?"

"No," Chase said.

"Start stealing cars again?"

Chase let it sit out there and didn't answer. Jonah chewed his eggs and bacon, watching him without watching him. He'd talk about the house money pretty soon, just to make sure Chase hadn't forgotten about his promise.

"Then what?" Angie said.

"It's not entirely over yet," he told her.

"No? What do you mean? What else is there?"

"One last shot," he said.

Jonah looked up. "Cleveland."

"Yeah."

Jonah shook his head, his eyes black and endlessly steady. "That's no help. They were running a game on that idiot."

"Yeah, but that piece of it rang true. The two crew members talking. One a little drunk, a little too loud. It sounded like a slip to me."

"Not to me. They're too good."

Chase shrugged.

"You still owe me a hundred grand."

"I know."

Angie fluffed the shoulders of her blouse. Chase was sure it was just so he'd take another look at her rack. It was a good head game, wearing Lila's clothes. Angie was young but she'd picked up a lot of hard-fought insight. Working with Jonah had just refined her own natural facility.

"Are you still with me on this?" Chase asked his grandfather.

"There isn't anything anymore. You had a thread and let it go. I told you that you were playing it wrong."

"Yeah, you did."

Chase stood and paid the check. He didn't say anything on the way back. He found himself in the rearview and thought that perhaps he had changed just enough to go the rest of the road alone.

*W*hen they got back to the house, Chase expected the old man to pack up and take off without another word. But Jonah sat on the couch and started watching the tapes again. Maybe he really did have a thing for Marisa Iverson.

Chase went out to the garage and worked on the Chevelle a little more. Fifteen minutes later Angie came out. She leaned against the passenger door and he heard the thump of the .25 clocking the metal. She watched him milking the carburetor and timing chain for every last second he could pull from it.

She said, "You get overzealous too."

"I like things clean."

Angie said, "You really going to pay him a hundred dred g's for doing nothing?"

"Yes."

She looked at him like he was an idiot, and said, "You're an idiot."

Chase let it slide. He was letting more and more slide and wondered when it would stop, and what would happen right after that.

"How much of a cut will you walk away with?" he asked.

"Full partners. I get half. But I can't walk away."

"You could always go back to Miami."

"I'll never go back to Miami."

"Then what are you complaining for?"

"Are you really as thick as you seem, or are you pretending?"

"I'm pretending."

She frowned and turned aside, and in profile Chase saw the surgery scars more prominently, but somehow he seemed to like them even more. It was a good metaphor—one minute you saw one thing, the next something else. It all depended on the light and the angle.

She was mad he was going to pay out and not get into an argument with Jonah, something that might lead to them pulling guns on each other. He wanted to ask her what the old man had done to turn her against him like this.

Had his grandfather been the one who'd given her the scars? He couldn't see Jonah as the jealous type and figured his grandfather would've let her walk away if she wanted to go. Did she have something on him? Or did she just not understand that Jonah wasn't like other men and wouldn't give a damn if she left? Did it all break down to her just thinking he'd be bitter if she dumped him, that he'd hunt her down and try to get her back? She fucked him but didn't know him.

Or maybe there was something else to it.

He asked, "Why do you stick with him if you hate him so much?"

"What makes you think I hate him?"

"Every word you say."

Her expression hardened. "Where else could I go?"

"You could go anywhere. Jonah doesn't care what happens to you."

"I know that."

"Then what's the problem."

"He won't let me take Kylie."

Chase got out from under the hood, thinking maybe he heard wrong with the engine humming. "Kylie?"

Nodding, Angie gave him a look that told him, This is why Jonah has to die. "Our daughter."

Stupid to think it, but the idea of Jonah having a kid kind of startled Chase. The fact that Chase's own father *was* Jonah's kid didn't seem to enter into it. He just couldn't see Jonah sticking around a child for long. Changing diapers, reading Dr. Seuss, all that. Was this any different because Angie was a partner in the bent life?

"She's twenty-four months," Angie said. "The

happiest baby in the world. Never cries, never frowns. Has a head of wild curly blond hair. Where she got it from, I have no idea. Dark eyes and golden hair. She walks and talks like a champion."

Chase thought, Does family get any stranger than this? He had a snuffed mother, a suicided father, a murdered wife, a heartless grandfather, and a two-year-old aunt. "Pictures?"

"I had to leave them in Aspen when things went south."

"Where is she?"

"In Sarasota with my sister, Milagro. Milly. She's three years older than me, has a kid of her own. I told you I left my aunt's house as soon as I could. She pretty much did the same. She got married to a professional surfer before she graduated high school. He doesn't have much brains, been smacked in the head with his board too often, but he's got a good heart and he likes children. He has to tour a lot, goes to Southern California, out to Hawaii, even Australia. But he makes good money and I left them with a wedge of cash to watch over Kylie. We go back to visit when we can, at least two or three times a year."

Chase stared at her. He toyed with the Chevelle's idle so the noise would drown their voices. He moved closer to her. "I still don't get it. So why don't you leave him?"

"He thinks it's important. Blood. Family. He'd let me go in half a second, but he'd never let me take Kylie."

It surprised Chase. He couldn't imagine Jonah ever caring so much about anything, except money.

Angie said, "He'd pull her out of my sister's house and take her along on scores, like he did with you."

"Don't let him."

"I won't."

It was always a gamble, being open and honest, in the straight life or the bent one. The knife was sharp enough to ease inside without you sticking your belly out to meet it. But they had somehow arrived at the place where the truth had to be spoken and had to be heard. He couldn't figure out how it had happened or why he was willing to take the risk. There was no reason at all, except he was thinking of the baby he and Lila had never had.

He said, "Is Jonah the one who beat the shit out of you so badly you needed the plastic surgery?"

"No."

"Would he ever hurt the kid?"

"No," Angie told him. "I don't know. Maybe. I can't be sure. I can't take the chance. Not with him. Not with my little girl."

He nodded, thinking, of course not. Where Jonah was concerned you could never take the risk. "I'll help however I can, but don't ever try to work me again like you did last night."

"All right."

"I won't kill him."

"Then you can't help me," she said.

"I can set you up with some cash."

"I've got cash. I can always get cash, but there isn't enough money in the world to make him quit coming after us."

It was true, and he'd have to think about that. If the old man really did think blood was important, what went on inside of him where Chase was concerned? Strange, but Chase wanted to know and he didn't want to know.

"Did Jonah ever really talk about me?"

"Yes. Mostly about the things I said. How good you were behind the wheel. How all the strings respected you even though you were so young. He did say he was sorry he didn't come to your wedding. I think he was touched that you'd invite him after not seeing him for all those years."

Jesus Christ, Chase just couldn't believe it. This had to be a setup. Probing Angie's gaze, he hunted for the slightest sign of a lie. He didn't find any. But there had to be more to it. He leaned back against the grille and let the thrum of the engine work into his chest, preparing him. "What else?"

"He thought about tracking you down and killing you after you left him. You actually managed to hurt him. You're lucky you ran. If he'd found you, you'd be dead and buried in some lime pit."

Chase worked on the car for another half hour after Angie left. He got the grease solvent, stepped inside, and washed up. The television was only a blue screen, the heist tape having run out.

Jonah said, "I'll make some calls. Maybe I can turn something up on this outfit."

"No."

"Why not?"

"You might call the wrong person. Someone you pissed off somewhere down the line who knows the crew and can alert them."

"So what? Maybe it'll rattle them. They're already gone. There's nothing left to lose."

"Are you in or out?"

"And I can say out and you'll still sell the house and pay me the money."

"We've been through that. Now it's time for you to tell me if you're still going to help me or not. If not, load up and go."

Chase thought about the crew and how loyal they'd been to one another. Marisa Iverson taking a beating, a gun to her head, and still not giving up the driver.

And here Chase was asking, repeatedly, after promising to pay a hundred k to his own blood, if his grandfather was going to help him. And the old man still not saying anything.

Jonah stared at him, dead-eyed. "I'll stay. But if you don't want me calling anyone, then how are you going to find out anything about these crew members who might've grown up in Cleveland?"

Chase said, "I'm going to talk to the cops."

When Chase walked into the squad room of Lila's old precinct he spotted Hopkins immediately. The cop was filling out forms on his desk, writing so slowly that it seemed the pen was hardly moving. He looked nervous, jumpy and pale, like he hadn't slept well in weeks. Chase could tell he'd been taken off active duty, probably because everybody including the police psychiatrist could see he was falling apart.

Chase wondered if he'd ever been a reliable partner for Lila. If for one stupid reason or another it was Hopkins who'd inadvertently made some mistake that had gotten her killed. The thought of it moved through him, gaining heat and strength, until his vision turned a gleaming red at the edges and his chest was tight.

"What are you doing here?" Hopkins said.

"I came to talk to Murray and Morgan."

"About what?"

"About whether they're making any progress tracking down the ice heisters."

Hopkins gave him a look that said he'd never really seen Chase before in his life. This wasn't a grease monkey schoolteacher in front of him anymore, and he was wondering where that guy had gone.

"If they had any information, I'm sure they would have phoned to let you know."

"Have you heard anything?"

"No."

Hopkins's body language gave off all the wrong signals. He smelled of peppermint gum and a hint of scotch, a pretty disgusting mix. No more fucking cake and coffee. Hopkins wasn't even slick enough to drink vodka on the job so that nobody would pick up on it. He was one of those mooks crying out to be caught and helped because he needed the attention. Chase felt a powerful wash of pity and loathing.

Scanning the desk, Chase noticed there were no photos. He pulled open the top drawer and Hopkins let out a frustrated grunt from the center of his chest. Inside the drawer were three framed photos of his wife and daughters, and a snapshot of Lila taken at one of the barbecues. The photo was ripped down the middle and Chase, who'd been sitting beside her, had been torn out.

He tapped the photo against the desktop, staring at Hopkins, trying to figure out if the guy was worth anything to him. Maybe he could still be put to use, or maybe Hopkins was too damaged for that now. He had to think about it.

With his lips crawling, Hopkins went, "Look, I've been meaning—"

Chase tossed the photo down, turned, and made his way to the other side of the room to where Murray and Morgan were each talking into a phone.

They both looked up at his approach and each of them frowned. He got close and listened in on their conversations. Murray was talking to his wife, telling her he was sorry he had come home so late last night and hadn't woken her the way she'd made him promise. But he had to put in the extra hours, the chief was breaking his ass. He pulled a face and glared at Chase, trying to spook him off. The vibe got ugly fast. That was all right. Chase continued standing there.

Good to see that Morgan was actually working the case. There was an intensity about him. He had two days of gray beard stubble and was bracing somebody hard over the phone, trying to get a line on somebody else. He scrawled in a notebook. He nodded, his chin bobbing. The next time he looked up at Chase he narrowed his eyes and tried to sort of climb away, hugging the phone to him. Chase stepped closer.

He was talking about some hooker and her pimp and a couple of gangbangers who'd hit a couple of banks in Roosevelt. It wasn't the right crew, but at least he was doing something. The cops would have a lot of misleading information. The manager of the diamond merchant's was in the morgue. Having Marisa's face on camera was worthless. Everything else would lead them to a dead end, and the aggravation would only get worse.

Murray told his wife he'd bring home her decongestant and hung up. He looked at Chase, sighed and said, "What can I do for you?" Doing the *Fuck off, twinky* thing again, but not having as much fun with it this time. He was tired and frustrated and seemed resigned to dealing with numerous pains in the ass this afternoon.

Might as well lay it on the line.

Chase asked, "Do you have any suspects who were born in or have some kind of a home base in Cleveland?"

"What?"

"Cleveland."

"Yeah, what about it?"

"You got anybody who might have been based there?"

"Why the hell are you asking about Cleveland for? What is this?"

Murray stood, stepped up, and tried to get in Chase's face. One heavy paw with a lot of liver spots lay on Chase's chest, pushing. Chase resisted, turned aside, and focused his gaze on Morgan.

Hanging up the phone, Morgan looked at him the same way that Hopkins had. With a lot of confusion and a little respect. He squinted at Chase, trying to get a bead on him. Raised his chin a little and scratched his stubble.

"You look like crap," he said.

"I haven't been sleeping much."

"Neither have we. What do you want?"

"A name," Chase said. "Or maybe two names. A husband-and-wife team? Possibly from Cleveland. Maybe working with another pro, also from there."

They remained like that for a solid minute. Morgan in his seat, staring, reading Chase's eyes and seeing something new. Murray with his hand on Chase's chest, intermittently attempting to shove him away, then relaxing. Then pressing. His aggression was almost a postscript. His wife was clogged.

They were three men of openly deep thoughts, saddled by convention, indignation, and a lack of results. This was Chase's last chance. He held his desperation inside and tried to plant it in the ice, keep it cool and under wraps, but he could still feel it trying to break free. His breathing grew deeper. The moment stretched. His vision grew red again. Murray shoved. Chase set his teeth and thought, Once more and I'm going to have to knock him down, and that will not be good at all.

"You stole the security tapes and file copies, didn't you?" Morgan asked.

"No," Chase said. He could barely see through the red.

Morgan said, "Sure you did," and started to go through his paperwork. He tossed manila folders aside, flipped through pages. "Cleveland. Not husband and wife, but brother and sister. Earl and Ellie Raymond. Grew up there, still have ties. Very sharp customers. They're heisters for certain, but they're nowhere near New York, so far as we know."

"They work with anybody with a scar on his forehead?"

Morgan stared even harder at him, tamping his teeth together, his wheels turning. Chase really didn't like that look.

Chase nodded, turning the name around in his head. Ellie Raymond. Murray backed away and said, "So what? We've got six sheets of suspects from all over the country. There's no more of a line on them than on a dozen other possibles." His tie was loose and he had ring around the collar. He turned to Chase and pointed a finger now, which was so much more accommodating than the palm in the chest. "You. You're trouble. I knew it first time I saw you—"

No wonder she wouldn't give up the driver. He was her brother.

"Thanks," Chase said and walked away.

On the other side of the squad room, he stopped off in front of Hopkins again. Since the guy was nothing but a desk jockey now, maybe he'd be bored or guilty enough to help. Chase couldn't entirely trust him but he couldn't trust anybody, so what the fuck.

Chase said, "My mother was murdered fifteen years ago. I want to check the case files."

"You'll have to send in the proper paperwork for a formal request, and you'll have to read the file at the courthouse records office in the company of an officer."

"Can you make copies?"

The question stumped Hopkins. Everything seemed to stump him. "I don't know."

"If you can't, steal them."

"What are you saying?" Hopkins's face opened up, his eyes wide but not quite as wide as they would've been if he wasn't drinking on the job. "I can't do that."

"Why not?"

"How am I supposed to steal records?"

"Slip them under your shirt, like you do with your flask of scotch."

Hopkins's expression buckled along its seams. "I don't know if I can do any of that."

He could feel Hopkins wanting to appease him. To be a friend, a buddy, a comrade. To do any damn thing to take his mind off his own misery. He wanted to throw back a few brews and talk about old times, except they didn't have any. More than that, he wanted Chase to tell him tales of Lila. Who knew how much she'd shared with the guy, but whatever it was, Hopkins needed more.

So put him to use.

Chase said, "Then go through them, work the case like you would any other. There's something wrong with how it was originally handled."

"How so?"

Chase thought, Besides the fact that they never caught who did it? He said, "I don't know, but maybe you'll spot it."

"My shift ends in an hour."

"Then do it tonight."

"I can't."

"You can get wasted afterward, Hopkins. Do this, and do it right. For Christ's sake, be a cop."

The tension rose. Chase had pushed him pretty hard today, and it looked like Hopkins might have had enough. His wife and kids were in the drawer for a reason. The corners of his mouth tightened and his eyes hardened for a moment, and then he went to pudding again. That didn't matter, so long as he got the job done.

"Listen, about Lila—"

Same way he'd phrased it last time, but with something a little different working to the surface now. His voice firmer, a bit rougher.

Chase waited. "What about her?"

"I just wanted to let you know . . . nothing ever happened between us."

Chase waited some more but that was apparently it. The guy revving himself up only to say that, like it was important. Pretending to come out with something of significance while he really held everything back.

Chase asked, "Your wife left you, didn't she? Took the kids?"

"Yes," Hopkins said. His breathing grew a touch more rapid, the peppermint-and-scotch aroma wafting to and fro. "How did you know that?"

"You're guilty for all the wrong reasons. I know there was nothing between you and Lila. She was my girl. You want to swoon over her photos, go right ahead. But I think you'd be better off straightening your ass up and getting your family back. Now, are you going to go check the files for me or what?"

Next step, Chase called the Deuce and gave him his credit card number again, told him to drop everything else, this was a rush.

Deucie called back three hours later. "Earl and Ellie Raymond. Live in Cleveland, play everyplace else. They're troublemakers. They're smart but a little too cowboy. Adrenaline junkies, they like it when they get into scrapes. They've put together strings with Kel Clarke, Slip Jenson, and Jason Fleischer. Those are the names I got."

"Any have a scar on his forehead?"

"Who the fuck knows? Like I go bowling with these assholes?"

"Which is the driver?"

"No idea. I never heard of any of them before. They're young, on a different circuit. This new breed, it's not about the money for them, it's just the juice of the action. With some fat, greedy bastard, you know he wants to get clear with the cash to spend it. This type? When they're not pulling scores they probably go do that whatchacallit with the cliffs, the freebasing . . . no, base-jumping."

"How about where they hole up?"

"All I heard was they use a fence in SoHo sometimes. Shonny Fishman. Has a pawnshop on West Broadway and Broome, I think. Or Spring. No, Broome. One of those. I know Shonny. Used to deal with him when I was first coming up. Little old Jew prick takes an extra two points off the top because he pays faster than the rest of the fences. The others, they won't go into their pocket and pay at once, takes time to spread the merchandise around, especially if it's got real heat on it. They pay out in six, twelve, maybe eighteen months. But Shonny, he's got a bankroll could choke the fuckin' Statue of Liberty. Takes him two or three weeks max. He's got four brothers and something like eight cousins, all of them shysters. A couple of them work in the D.A.'s office, so he's got good protection. If the shit ever comes down, he'll fade to Israel and buy himself a McDonald's franchise in Tel Aviv."

"Is there a cage I need to be buzzed through?"

"Of course there's a cage. Everybody's got cages now. You know that."

He didn't know that. It meant he might need his tools to pull this off. "What do I say to show him I'm not there to buy a saxophone or a brooch for my grandmother?"

"How the hell should I know? I never had to hock a Rolex with him. Well, not since the Heidi Bowl, I lost my fuckin' shirt that day. Anyway, you'll figure it out. And try not to kill him, I always kinda liked Shonny."

"No promises," Chase said.

He called information and got the number for Fishman's Loan Society and Trading Depot. Jesus Christ, pawnbrokers really went all out with naming their places, Shonny and Bookatee would've gotten along just groovy.

Shonny picked up and Chase asked what time he'd be closing. Shonny Fishman spoke with a rich and mannered voice. "Eight o'clock tonight, thank you for phoning."

Chase laid it out for his grandfather and Jonah said, "They'll be somewhere close to him. Probably in Jersey. They make a run into the city, grab their parcels of the payout, then go back and wait until the next one is due. If the crew hasn't already broken up, they soon will. A couple will scatter with their caches and pick up the rest of their pay somewhere down the line. There's five in the crew but maybe we'll get lucky and a couple will have peeled off."

They still had a few hours to kill. Angie had taken the van and gotten enough groceries to cook dinner. Chase sensed she was trying to be accommodating, maternal in whatever way she could considering the circumstances. Jonah didn't notice. She tried to make small talk but Chase was too wrapped up in his own thoughts. He ate mechanically and tried to put his eyes anywhere except on Lila's photos. He kept hearing her telling him not to do this.

Angie cleaned her gun again and started selecting others from Lila's spread. Chase got out Marisa Iverson's—no, he had to start thinking of her under her real name, Ellie Raymond, drive it in, *Ellie Raymond*—Ellie Raymond's 9mm. Lila had extra ammo out in the cabinet in the garage and he pocketed two clips, and put several more in his knapsack.

He told Angie, "You don't need to come along."

"What?"

He said, "Stay here."

"I'm a full partner, remember?"

"You'll get your share."

"Who said anything about that?" she asked.

Jonah said, "She's coming."

Chase shook his head. "I'm calling the play."

"Not if you want it done right. Not this one, with my neck on the line. She comes along."

"Your kid needs a mother."

The fact that Chase knew about Kylie didn't faze Jonah in the slightest. He ignored it. "We need at least a third person if we're really going after this crew. There's five of them. Even if we get the drop, we're at a disadvantage. We'll need to hit them hard and fast. We need firepower, and she's a good shooter."

"I am," Angie said.

"I believe you," Chase told her. "It's not about that; aren't you listening?"

Jonah stared hard and Chase knew why. It was stupid for him to have suddenly gotten soft, right now as they were heading out to finish this thing. But he couldn't help it. He kept thinking of the two-year-old girl. There were enough lost children in his life already. His dead unborn sibling who had been taken out of the game before taking its first breath. The child he and Lila wanted and couldn't have. The need for a kid was still all around him, rising within him. He might not have done anything else right, but he could make the effort to allow Kylie to be raised by her own mother.

Looking at Jonah he knew he might've already gone too far. His grandfather stood there, hard, mean, staring at Chase, who wasn't hard enough or mean enough despite wanting to snuff the driver. He couldn't make any sense of it himself, and Jonah, who didn't put up with shit like this, was no more than a cunt hair away from going for his gun.

All right, maybe he'd fucked up, but he kept his eyes on the old man, letting him know, If you want it to be now, I'm ready.

Angie said, "Let's go, it's settled. I'm coming

along." She grabbed Chase by the arm. "You drive, it's what you do best."

On the Southern State Parkway, letting the Chevelle run just a little wild, shredding to ninety and then easing it back down to sixty, he asked his grandfather, "Were you really going to try to heist the rez casino?"

"You're pretty fixated on that."

"I can't figure out any other reason why you'd be up in White Plains."

"Even if the casino is owned by Indians, there's got to be some mob kickback."

"You were going to score some bagman? Isn't that more trouble than it's worth, getting on the mob's bad side?"

"The syndicate's been fighting among itself pretty seriously the past couple of years."

Chase remembered thinking that after the Deuce told him a don's son was looking for a wheelman. "Why?"

"Happens every twenty years or so, when the bosses get ready to retire and turn the reins over to their oldest sons. All their wingmen and con-siglieres start feeling ripped off and make a play. Either they cap the don's kid or they get aced after long service, which leaves the families even weaker. So the other mob crews start sniffing around, seeing if they can pick the meat from the bones, and then they start going to war over the juiciest pieces."

"And you go in for the scraps."

"Sure."

The Southern State turned into the Belt Parkway and twenty minutes later they were crossing the Brooklyn Bridge. It would land them at the bottom of Manhattan practically on top of Fishman's Loan Society and Trading Depot.

The feel of the city started to bring back memories. All the shows he and Lila had taken in. The times down at the South Street Seaport, looking out over the waves. Lila beating the crap out of the kid who'd tried to boost her wallet in the Penn Station waiting room. The hotel room where he'd helped to wipe down fingerprints, tossing butts in the john while Walcroft kicked open the closet door.

Chase said, "Tell me what happened down in Philly, with you and Rook and Buzzard Allen. How'd you get talked into trying to steal Renaissance paintings?"

Jonah's mouth barely moved. "You're in a talkative mood."

"No," Chase said. "I just want answers."

"The Philly museum heist isn't an answer to anything you want to know."

"You're right."

You didn't break into it slowly, there was no point. It was how normal people talked, not the way Jonah did.

"Then what are you pushing on about?" his grandfather asked.

Shutting his eyes, Chase ticked off three seconds, letting the car guide and strengthen him.

"What did Walcroft do?" he asked. "He wasn't wired. So why'd you really ace him?"

Now, Jonah doing what he did best, giving back nothing at all unless it hurt. "He grabbed that tuna. Nobody needs a joker like that on a job."

They sat at the curb outside the pawnshop in SoHo, watching Shonny Fishman through the bars of his front window. There were still three people in the store doing business. Shonny was smiling broadly, so something was working out for him in there.

Chase checked his watch. They still had about twenty minutes before Shonny would pack it in for the night.

Hopkins phoned and said, "I went to the Hall of Records and dug through your mother's case. They had no serious suspects but set their sights on your dad, of course."

"No prints or witnesses or anything?"

"No. I don't know what you think is wrong here. I mean, I can't find anything that sticks out. Your father was watched for a while because he acted so crazy afterward. They had surveillance on him for a couple weeks full-time, then off and on for a couple more after that. Says here he took you to your mother's grave every day, even in blizzards? And that he actually gave you liquor. You were, what, ten years old? Jesus Christ."

Chase thought of those long, terrible days at his mother's grave, his father unconscious in the snow, and Chase drunk with ice in his hair, trying to keep his dad warm. The cops had been watching and nobody had bothered to help him. He tried to clamp down on the sick feeling pouring through him. "Forget that."

"They almost dragged him in for it, but I guess they figured he'd suffered enough and wanted to cut a deal instead."

Reaching out, Chase touched the steering wheel, finding a cool authority in it. "What deal?"

"They let him walk so long as he would persuade you to go on television and make the plea to the killer."

"What?" His father had told him that he'd been approached by a newscaster to make the appeal, and the newscaster thought Chase should do it instead. "So it wasn't his idea."

"No, did you think it was?"

"Anything else?"

Hopkins's voice became charged with delight. "Oh, and I called my wife. We're going to have dinner and try to work things out. I think she—"

Chase hung up.

Jonah said, "What is it?"

"Nothing."

"Those were the last customers." Angie gestured from the backseat. "The place is empty now."

"Yeah."

"He'll be closing up soon. If you go in too late, he'll know it's a smash."

Chase had the 9mm and his tools in the pockets of his jacket. He slid out of the Chevelle and Jonah did the same.

The trouble would be the buzz gate. Shonny Fishman had dealt with thieves for too long not to recognize a couple right off. He'd never let them in. Even if they tapped on the security glass with the guns and acted like they'd shoot their way in, Shonny would just lam it out the back door or pick up a shotgun and blast them like fish in a barrel. Chase knew he'd have to pop the buzz gate.

He hit the door and got his tools out. He was still a little rusty, but after breaking into James Lefferts's home, Ellie Raymond's place, and the Nicholson house, he figured he could slip the gate in twenty or thirty seconds.

He told Jonah, "Block the view as much as you can."

His grandfather moved beside him and started talking loudly, smiling, acting drunk. It'd make Shonny Fishman roll his eyes and be reluctant to buzz them in, but at least he wouldn't be spooked yet. Jonah had perfect teeth even though he hardly ever showed them. His laugh was boisterous and booming. He was bullshitting about winning two grand on the game tonight. He didn't mention what kind of game or who the teams might be, because who the hell knew, but he sold it well. The laughter would sound very real to anybody else, but hearing it sent a spike through Chase's spine.

Under his breath, Jonah said, "Smart fucker, he's not buying it anymore," and the door popped.

One second the gun was hidden and the next it was in his hand as Jonah rushed inside and pointed it in Shonny Fishman's face. He moved Shonny from behind the counter. He kept close, the gun tight in Shonny's stomach so that no one could peer through the front window and catch what was going on.

Shonny had a bald head ringed by short white hair and covered with caramel-colored freckles and liver spots, a face like an old basset hound that just wanted to stay under the porch. He was short but wiry, with a kind of stable fortitude that would always get him through. The gun annoyed him more than it frightened him.

He said almost casually, "Damn it. I knew you two were up to something. That was very slick. That security gate cost me almost five grand."

"You need an upgrade," Chase told him.

"Security tapes," Jonah said. There were at least two cameras trained on them.

Shonny sighed. "Under the counter."

Most pawnshops would have the taping

equipment in the back, running all the time. But Shonny's other customers wouldn't be happy with that. They'd want to see him shut everything off and erase the tapes right in front of them, so he kept the gear close and up front. Jonah motioned Shonny aside and Chase slid behind the counter, shut the equipment down, and popped the tapes.

Chase knew guys like Shonny cared more about their money than their own lives or the lives of their friends. It was a kind of sickness, but there it was, and half the guys he'd ever run into in the bent life were pretty much the same. So Chase wanted to appeal to him fast.

He said, "Shonny, we're not here for your cash. We could tap-dance around each other for twenty minutes, but I'm all out of patience and time. I want Earl and Ellie Raymond. You deal with them. You still must have some payout for them from the double diamond merchant score. Just give me where they're holed up and you might walk away from this."

"'Might walk away?' From guys like you two? You're lying to a dead man, and I'd say that's simply unforgivable."

"Maybe you missed the frenzy in my voice, Shonny." Chase brought the butt of the gun down across Shonny's bald head and opened a gash up. It wasn't too hard a shot, but head wounds were notorious bleeders, and already there was a pint leaking down Shonny's slightly aggrieved face.

Yanking him up by his collar, Chase stuck the

barrel of the 9mm under Shonny's chin. "Might walk away's about as good as you're going to get from me, and the longer you make me wait, the thinner your chances get. So how about it?"

You had to give it to him, he was holding on. Some of these old-timers, they figured they had one foot in the grave already so figured they could tell anybody to fuck off. "What do you want with them?"

"I want to sell them some aluminum siding," Chase said and dug the gun in farther until Shonny let out an ugly "glckk" noise. He lashed his head to the side and a swathe of blood splashed against the floor.

Now maybe they'd get somewhere. Shonny Fishman held out another minute and said, "121 Pine Drive in Smithtown, out on the Island."

That was Marisa Iverson's—Ellie Raymond's—address, the house Chase had broken into.

"You prick." Chase smacked him in the head again with the barrel of the gun. Shonny cried out but not enough.

All right, it had to be done. Chase worked the guy's ribs with four fast body blows. No matter how tough you thought you were, a broken rib would change your goddamn mind.

It happened so quick that Shonny Fishman didn't even scream. He hacked up pink phlegm and started to slide to the floor, but Jonah propped him against the counter.

"Listen, Shonny," Chase said. "I respect your

loyalty, courage, determination, and all that. But next I'm going to shoot off your johnson. I'm not going to kill you, get it? You're not going to die. But I'll leave you in a very bad ugly mess, and even an old bastard like you doesn't want to piss through a tube, right? So, in case you missed it, I don't want your money. In this world, that makes me as righteous a soul as you've ever met. Now, where are they?"

Shonny Fishman's eyes were brimming with worry now. Even if he wasn't getting laid regularly or couldn't get it up anymore a guy still liked to know he had a pecker.

Putting the barrel of the 9mm to Shonny's crotch, Chase said, "It's time. Where are they?"

"Foundry Street."

"Newark?"

"It's a run-down motel. I don't know which number room they're in."

"How many? Who's there?"

"Ellie and Earl and Slip."

The Deuce had mentioned that name. "Slip Jenson. He have a scar on his forehead?"

Shonny had to use his knuckles to clear the blood from the corner of his eyes. "Yeah. The others, I don't know their names, but they took their share of the initial payout and went to A.C. to blow it on hookers and Texas Holdem. That's what Earl said."

That didn't matter unless one of them was the driver. Chase had to be sure. "Now just one more thing. Who's the getaway man for their crew?"

"Earl. Earl does all the driving."

There it was.

Checking out the counter to see if there were any watches or rings he might want to pocket, Jonah said, "If you don't ace him, he'll call them and they'll run again."

Finally, that got Shonny truly scared. Jonah could do it to you, no matter how solid you were. Shonny started waving his hands, jittering in place. "Wait wait, listen to me, you don't have to do anything. I'm no trouble to you—"

The cold spot beckoned. Chase slid into it. He was hard and he was cool. Cool enough to know you didn't snuff some prick just because he'd done business with the guy you really wanted. He couldn't lose focus on the driver.

"Let's go in the back."

"I told you, I'm not a threat! You don't have to do this!"

"Shonny, you get all uptight at the worst times."

He slugged Shonny across the back of the head, a blow he figured would keep the guy unconscious for a few hours. It would be all over by then, one way or another. He could feel that now.

The icy breeze in the cold spot whispered the truth to him. There was an understanding about death and murder and the extent of blood and heartache. How grief could drive you out of your head, the way it threatened to do with him right now, the way it had done with his father. He had to hold steady.

Jonah said, "You're still playing it wrong."

Chase dragged Shonny Fishman to his back room. There was another cage back there full of jewelry and other high-end items he didn't leave out front on the floor. He got Shonny's keys out, tossed the guy inside, and started to close the gate. Jonah stepped forward and pulled a canvas bag from underneath his jacket. He cleaned the shelves and slammed the gate shut.

On their way out he threw the tapes in the bag too.

They walked to the Chevelle and Angie was in the driver's seat. Chase glared at her and she slid away into the back. She'd played it smart. She'd been prepared in case something went wrong and they had to bolt out of there fast. But you never got behind the wheel of another driver's car. Unless you were stealing it.

Chase pulled away from the curb and drove like a little old lady up through SoHo, heading for the Holland Tunnel. The engine wanted to scream. So did he.

*N*ot *even nine-thirty yet and the motel manager's of-*fice was locked. It was that kind of a place. Nobody needed to spend a night over in this part of Newark unless they were blowing through on a job or looking for a twenty-minute hooker. The manager would be some old man off getting a few beers around the block. He'd be back on deck in a half hour and then he'd go off again when he got too bored. The whores wouldn't be out in full swing until midnight when they started pulling over tricks on the turnpike or Route 9a. It had once been a residential area and a few dilapidated houses remained. Foundry Street was a dead road in a dead part of a dying city.

Chase popped the door and checked the wall where the room keys were set on hooks. The motel hadn't upgraded to computerized cards and never

would. They'd raze the place first. Seven rooms
were currently in use.

He drove slowly through the parking lot peering through the slits between drapes. He spotted
some addicts getting wasted, a couple of teenagers
watching television getting ready to jump each
other, and some drunks with nowhere else to go.
Only two rooms had the drapes completely drawn.
They were side by side. Chase backed into a spot
directly across from them.

He looked for a car that had some real muscle
to it but couldn't spot anything a wheelman would
drive. That meant Earl Raymond either parked off
site, wasn't here at the moment, or the crew had already moved on.

"If they're here, they'll be in one of those two
rooms," Jonah said.

Angie had one of Lila's .32s on her now, not
quite as small as the Bernadelli but in a tight,
closed room you wouldn't need much more than
that. "Or maybe both."

"That means we have to go into both, at the
same time," Jonah said. "If you hadn't left the
pawnbroker alive we could've taken more time
and checked things over for as long as we needed
to. But this has to end tonight."

"I want it to end tonight," Chase told him.

"If you're still in a talkative mood, get over it
now. We go in fast and hard. You ice them or
they'll ice us. They've been smarter than you so far

because you haven't wanted to take this all the way. Are you ready to do that now?"

"Yes."

Angie's current was riding a little high. Chase could feel her ramped in the backseat. He found her eyes in the rearview and felt a flush of shame for having dragged her into this mess. The old man owed him but she didn't. He wanted to tell her that she should stay behind, but he knew she'd just give him the whole full-partner spiel again. He didn't want her baby daughter to grow up without a mother, stuck with a father like Jonah.

Jonah kept watching Chase another few seconds, trying to read the truth. Finally he turned away and said to Angie, "You ready?"

"Yep."

"Let's go."

It was difficult turning the engine off. Chase pocketed the keys and felt the brutal weight of Ellie Raymond's 9mm against his body. He thought, This isn't how it should be. I just want the driver. Me and Earl, we should be doing this one on one, with nothing else except our cars. We should rip through the night shredding road, our tires smoking. We should get it up to triple digits and haul ass along empty highways, alone except for the engine and the radio.

Chase tried to hit the cold spot but every time he did he found Lila there, filling it with warmth.

Not much of a plan, really. Jonah took the room to the left, #19, and Chase the one to the right,

#18. He got out his tools. He thought they should count to three and do it together, but before he could start he heard Jonah abruptly breaking down the door. So it was like that. No time to slip the lock.

Chase kicked the door in on #18. It wasn't as easy to break down doors as they made it look in the movies. It hurt and it threw him off a step. Now he was three—four seconds behind, and by the time he got his bearings he saw, with a mixture of relief and revulsion, that he'd found them. Ellie Raymond and two men were inside, scrambling for their weapons.

And goddammit, his grandfather had been right. Chase still *was* in a talkative mood. He had things to say. The world sped up around him and he was fast enough to meet it, but he couldn't get out all that was inside him. He heard gunfire next door and wondered if the other guys on the string had come back from Atlantic City early or if Jonah had walked into a drug deal or some shit like that. Ellie Raymond was bending forward, and Chase finally got a good look at her without the disguise. Lovely, firm, vicious, cool and cold, radiant with her lips flattened but her eyes alive with joy. She was an adrenaline junkie, she wanted it rough and wild. She recognized him and let out a heartwarming giggle. The sound of it knifed through his chest. His gaze slid sideways and he saw one of the men moving, digging for a gun under the bed. These people, they all had pistols clipped to the

bed frames, they all wanted to cap whoever might
fuck them. The guy looked a little scared, worried.
His face was flat and ugly, and he had a terrible scar
on his forehead. Slip Jenson. Chase checked the
other guy and knew, right then, there, that's him,
that's Earl, the mad-dog shooter, the driver. The
guy was smiling, sure. He was all flash. He was
handsome as hell, a hard-stepper like his sister, taking it as rough as he could because he liked it that
way. Chase wanted to talk but had no idea what to
say. Maybe he wanted to ask them their story, what
made them this way. They all had their hands on
their pistols now. If he couldn't talk to Earl then
they should at least meet each other's eyes, make
that connection, where they both understood that
this is the moment to settle all accounts. But Earl
was looking at Chase's chest, bringing up a Glock.
The Jonah in Chase's head said, Fucking shoot
them already. The Lila in his head told him,
Sweetness, it's time, it's time. Of course it was.
Chase started firing and so did they.

It happened fast.

The room was small but large enough for two double beds, with a nightstand between them. Earl was behind the bed farthest away, Ellie between the two, Slip Jenson closest to Chase, so he was the one Chase popped first, even though he didn't have anything against the guy. Jenson's flat, ugly face got even flatter and much uglier, exploding in a cloud of gristle and bone chips. Chase went down for cover, but Ellie Raymond had her gun hand propped up on the mattress and she shot at Chase as he was moving. The bullet took him high in the right side, spun him around, and took a chunk of meat out from just under his ribs. She'd clipped the lung. He didn't feel it yet but knew he would soon. Already his breathing changed and he had to suck wind. Chase fell on top of Slip Jenson's corpse and the dead man spit blood across Chase's throat.

Ellie Raymond was taking the fight to him. She dove on top of the bed, firing twice, three times, the bullets tearing up the carpet around him. He thought, How could she miss me? Then he realized this was her weakness. She wanted the juice to last so she stretched the action out.

The next one caught him in the lower leg and this time he felt it immediately and he couldn't help but cry out. It made her toss off another giggle. Still grinning, Earl spoke one word. "Don't."

So maybe he wasn't quite as crazy as his sister, or maybe he just didn't want her to go it alone like this.

Chase stuck his arm under the bed and fired twice up through the mattress and heard Ellie scream.

He rolled and went for a different angle, trying for Earl across the room now. Earl dogged it into the bathroom, slammed the door, and Chase heard glass shattering.

All of this, and the fucker runs for it and leaves his own sister behind. Ellie showed such loyalty for this? Chase wondered if she'd understand her brother had left her to die.

He tried to stand but his wounded leg wouldn't support him and he went down again. Son of a bitch. He made the effort again and managed to keep on his feet. He checked Ellie Raymond, laid out across the bed on her back. She was gut-shot and panting, her face slathered in sweat.

"That's my gun," she said, holding her bubbling stomach, her face tight with pain.

"Yeah," he said, his voice strange because there wasn't enough wind in it.

"I thought you didn't like guns."

"I don't," he gasped, and shot her twice in the heart.

Weird feeling, having only one lung inflate. Not enough air getting through. Felt like he was slowly drowning. Chase stepped out the door and checked Room #19. There was a businessman with no pants on cowering on the bed with an enormous naked black hooker sitting next to him.

Jonah was sitting in a pool of blood at the foot of the bed. He'd been shot in the back twice but his face didn't register much pain.

Angie was lying just inside the room, dead. Most of her face had been torn off and flung onto the wall behind her. Chase could see what had happened. She'd made a move on the old man, trying to get out from under him. She'd put two into him and still hadn't been able to put him down, and Jonah had killed her.

"Jesus fucking Christ," Chase hissed.

And in Jonah's face, even now, after clipping the woman who had been like his wife, the mother of his kid, the old man showed nothing. He said, "Give me a hand."

"In a minute. It's not over yet."

Chase moved away, took three steps out the door, and fell on his face.

Lila was there. She came to him and gripped the sides of his face and raised his head. She said, "I didn't want any of this for you, but we're in it now. You've got to get up, love, he's coming."

A shriek of tires erupted from around the corner of the far end of the parking lot. Chase opened his eyes and tried to rouse himself. Earl must've parked his muscle in one of the driveways of the decrepit houses around them. A gutsy move being that far away from your wheels. Chase saw a flash of headlights reflected in the windows of the manager's office a moment before Earl's car appeared.

So they were going to get to race after all.

Chase stumbled out to the Chevelle and saw that Earl Raymond was driving a gorgeous 1970 Plymouth Superbird with the funky extended front end but without the high back spoiler. It was tuned up right. The 440 V8 damn near howled.

Earl slowed and came to a stop in the distance, checking the scene, trying to squeeze a little more action from it.

Settling behind the wheel of the Chevelle and splashing blood over the seat, Chase twisted the key and felt the power of the engine rise into him.

The Chevelle was ready. Its dark energy merged with his own.

He thought, This is how it's supposed to be. Both of us in machines, ready to go running around the city. Or just sit back and play chicken, do this short and sweet.

Seventy yards separated them. No chance to build up any real speed, but still, there'd be enough.

They could play tag through Jersey, ripping up these roads, wheeling through residential neighborhoods, and breaking for the highway. They might shake and bump each other for hours, crushing car frames and bouncing loose the suspension, the exhaust systems, mile after mile. Earl occasionally hanging his left arm out and firing mad-dog style.

Where would they end up? The Pine Barrens? Atlantic City? Philly? Mississippi? Would either of them want it to end or would it just be too much fun letting the hammer down and running like that for the remainder of their lives?

Chase thought, This is what he's thinking too. I can feel it.

Earl revved his engine. Such an old-school thing to do, but he probably couldn't help himself. His stereo was turned all the way up, a nice speaker system pounding out an incredible bass track that pummeled the night. He was having a ball. Chase wasn't. He was leaking out across the floor mat.

He waited. The Chevelle's power burned through

him. It worked into his bones, into the back of his skull, rattling away some of the pain but none of the rage.

Earl Raymond had killed Lila and Chase still wanted to talk to him, pull photos from his wallet, stick them in Earl's face and get some kind of human reaction from him. At least hear his voice, the nuances, the inflections. Watch his eyes. Earl stood on the brake and the gas pedal together, the tires screeching insanely, smoking like a brush fire had been set underneath the Superbird. He dropped off the brake and tore at Chase, eating the space between them.

Chase moved into the cold spot. It frosted his burning mind. He saw what he had to do.

He opened the door and climbed out.

He walked away from the Chevelle.

A driver without any muscle but with plenty of drive. Chase doubled over and let out Walcroft's noise. Then he straightened himself as his blood hit the asphalt.

He stood his ground as the Plymouth ripped toward him, edging past 30 mph, 40, 50. Earl hung his left arm out the window and blasted away.

A bullet took Chase in the collarbone and his right arm went dead. But he didn't drop the gun.

He reached for it with his left and had to pry the numb fingers of his right hand from around the pistol.

There was still time, he could do this. He was fast. Even now, sounding like a busted bellows, his chest heaving. He closed his fist around the 9mm and lifted his left arm and started firing.

The Plymouth was so damn close now, the blazing headlights illuminating Chase with an icy intensity that met with his own inner cool. He fired blindly five times.

He missed. The grille was less than thirty feet away, the car hauling in at about sixty. Time maybe for one last pull of the trigger, or maybe not. The world was nothing but light. He snapped a final shot off.

Now the front end was no more than ten feet away, and Chase was going to die beneath three thousand pounds of Detroit muscle. It actually made him grin.

Earl cared for the car but wasn't overzealous about it. If he had been, he would've restored it fully and put the funky back spoiler on even if it did make the Superbird stand out. He didn't quite love the car enough.

There was a slight pull to the right and the Plymouth angled just enough to miss Chase as it roared past.

He got a good look. The last bullet had smashed Earl's head apart and a nice red cascade had covered the dashboard and the inside of the windshield.

The Superbird's side mirror caught Chase's left hand and he felt three of his fingers break. It spun him around and he polished the driver's door with the seat of his pants. He went down again and watched the car make a wild turn and plow into the front of Room #18, roaring over and crushing the bodies of the crew. The idle was stuck high and the engine kept screaming. Chase wanted to join it, but the Jonah in his head said, Get the fuck up.

His grandfather was there telling him, "Get the fuck up."

Jonah drove like shit. Chase could see why the old man always needed a getaway driver, and why during the Philly museum heist escape he'd nearly run over a teenage girl. Way too loose with the wheel, too heavy on the gas pedal, taking turns too tight. He swerved all over the road trying to get to the George Washington Bridge. Maybe the two bullets in his back had something to do with it, but still.

Clearly Jonah still knew his way around the area but not as well as Chase did, and the old man kept barking questions, asking if he should take a left or right here to get uptown, which way was quickest to the East Side. Chase tried to focus and keep his eyes on the road but his vision kept doubling, tripling. Racking coughs filled his mouth with blood. Even then, he couldn't brush past the nagging feeling that he was staining the seat. The next thief who boosted the Chevelle was going to have his work cut out for him when it came to the detailing.

Way uptown on 203rd, right on the Harlem River, Jonah finally got them to a safe doctor, which meant the guy was a fucking butcher. He was also a junkie and looked high on speed or meth. He'd fallen from grace decades ago and stared vacantly but bright-eyed at Chase. The guy looked happy and genuinely deranged.

He gave Chase a needle and said, "This will kill the pain."

It didn't. Five minutes later, while the guy poked around in the bullet wounds, scratching at the collarbone, Chase wailed as loudly as he could, which wasn't much above a whisper because of the collapsed lung. He tried to reach his good hand out to Jonah but the arm was nearly useless. Still, Jonah knew what Chase was doing, and Chase was surprised as hell when his grandfather took it. That meant something but he wasn't sure what.

The doctor yanked on Chase's arm and leg and felt around his ribs. No bones had been broken except for the fingers. The bullets had gone straight through. The doctor said he was lucky. Not much muscle damage. But the blood loss. The chance for infection. The lung. He got out needles and tubes and shoved them into Chase's chest.

You get shot three times and somebody still has to come along and put more holes in you. Chase didn't feel lucky. The doctor leaned forward and clasped the tube between his lips and started to blow. Chase felt his lung expanding but was suddenly worried about what kind of germs this dude was breathing into him. Chase vomited from the pain and passed out.

He dreamed of his sibling who had never been born. The baby sat at the kitchen table in a high chair. Chase couldn't tell if it was a boy or a girl. The kid knew more answers than he did. The kid had been there the day his mother had been murdered and had died with her. Chase asked questions he couldn't hear. The kid responded in Chase's own voice, going, You already know all that, don't you?

Once he came awake for only a few seconds and saw the doctor working on Jonah's back, the old man's skin and muscle held open by retractors. There was blood everywhere. His grandfather didn't make a sound, the hard son of a bitch. It seemed impossible.

Now that the driver was iced, Chase realized that Jonah hadn't done much in the way of helping him at all. He'd punched in the wrong door and wound up acing his own woman, leaving Chase to take down the three crew members by himself.

He whispered, "You know, you didn't do shit."

With the doc drilling for bullets around the old man's spine, Jonah said, "You were two minutes from being dead when I got you here. Does that count?"

With a sluggish anger trying to overcome him, Chase wanted to say, Fuck no, that wasn't the job, but he was already unconscious.

The next time he woke he was bandaged, his hand was in a cast, and he could barely move, but the painkillers had finally kicked in because he didn't feel much. There were drains all over him. He was hooked to a couple of IVs and a blood bag. He didn't even want to think about where the blood had come from. Jonah was sitting up staring out the window, where you could just make out the Grand Concourse in the Bronx across the river to the east.

Jonah said, "You've been out for two and a half days. Doc says you'll be okay if your heart doesn't stop."

"Terrific."

"Go easy on the lung."

Chase had to wonder, How the hell do you go easy on a lung? No scuba diving? No marathons? No deep breaths? He tried to struggle up but nothing would work right.

His grandfather said, "It'll be a couple more days before you can be moved."

"How much is he costing us?"

"Nothing, I did a favor for him once."

That made no sense. Jonah never did favors.

All it meant was he'd crossed up with the doc at one point and hadn't killed him. "What's he on?"

"I'm not sure. Coke, maybe."

"What's he know about us?"

"He doesn't know anything about anything," Jonah said. "That's why we can come to him."

Sleep drew Chase down again, but he fought the tide, knowing he needed to think a few things through. Morgan and Murray would be on to him now. He'd practically lit the sky with a blazing neon arrow pointing to himself. Still, he didn't think they'd press him too hard, but you never knew. Who cared exactly how a cop killer got taken down? They were macho hard-asses, they might like that Chase had handled this himself even if there were four bodies left behind. They could juggle the paperwork, take some of the credit for it, get their photos in the papers with some of the gropers. He figured Morgan would let it slide, but Murray might be trouble. It didn't matter much, one way or the other. He'd done what had to be done, and if he had to go on the run with them chasing behind him, or if he wound up in the can for twelve to fifteen, or if they got him in a corner and made him draw, he'd do it for his girl.

Four days later, on the way home, lying in the back-seat and still smelling the oil from Angie's Bernadelli subcompact, Chase asked the old man, "Does it bother you that you she made a play?"

Jonah, too heavy on the gas, barreling through traffic on the parkway, said, "I expected it."

"Why?"

"I always expect it."

"Yeah, but do you ever understand it?"

Jonah caught his eyes in the rearview. The car shimmied. The old man hardly looked at the road, like he thought there would never be a curve ahead. "It happened once before. And for the same reason. Over a kid."

"What? With who?"

"Another foolish woman."

"Yeah, but who?"

Jonah said nothing for miles. Then, "Are you going to try me?"

"What?"

"She asked you to, didn't she?"

"Why didn't you just let her go?"

"She could've left anytime. But I need Kylie. Blood is important."

As if the names on his scarred arms actually meant anything. "Since when?"

"Forever."

"Do you love anything?"

The old man's gaze held him in the mirror. You could spend your whole life trying to figure out what Jonah knew about love and grief, and you'd never get an answer.

Chase thought he should've tried harder to

help Angie, to dissuade her from taking a run at
Jonah, at least with a .32. Maybe a .44. Maybe
Chase should've drawn on him. Yanked a gun or
thrown at least one good punch if nothing else.
Whatever happened afterward, it might've been
worth it.

But then he remembered his grandfather gripping his hand in the doc's office. That meant
something. Anyone else, you might say it was a
gesture of the heart. But the old man would always
be beyond him. And always inside of him.

Jonah didn't plan to stay. He packed the van with his gear and kept pulling out whatever belonged to Angie and leaving it on the side of the garage. There wasn't a lot. The little pile became a slightly larger little pile as he added a belt, a scarf. All that was left of the woman's history, besides her child somewhere in Florida, could be fit into a shoe box.

Popping a handful of pills the doc had given him, Chase swallowed them dry. Painkillers and antibiotics, but they didn't seem to be doing much good so far. He'd reached his limit and was covered in cold sweat. His bandages had soaked through and needed changing.

He leaned against the hood of the Chevelle, almost ready to drop, staring up at his grandfather through his damp hair.

Jonah said, "It's a nice house. You shouldn't sell it."

"It's over for me here. I'm leaving."

"Any idea where you'll go?"

"No," Chase said. "But I'll get you your money."

"Forget that."

Chase had been through a lot these last few weeks, but his grandfather's voice now, the words he spoke, nearly took out his knees. He wavered. "What?"

"After what I nabbed from Fishman the fence and scored off the crew, I made out all right."

"The crew? When did you score them?"

"There was ninety grand in the closet of their motel room," Jonah said.

"When did you have a chance to dig around in their room?"

"Before I pulled you out of there."

Which meant that while Chase was dying in the lot bleeding out, and everyone in the crew was dead, and the Superbird was still roaring with a corpse's foot jammed down on the pedal, the car wedged into the front of the room having crashed through the wall, Jonah had staggered around with two in the back after having just killed the mother of his child and dug among the bodies to find the cash.

The old man had finished packing the van.

He got to the door and said, "You know how to get in touch with me if you need to."

Same thing he'd said ten years ago when they'd split up.

And then his grandfather pulled out of the garage and drove off past the Nicholsons' house and was just as gone.

The Jonah inside Chase's head said, Don't ever trust me. I'm going to kill you one day.

The weakness overpowered him for the next two days, but the next morning he felt much stronger. He got out of bed and cleaned up the blood in the Chevelle. He took more of the pills the doc had given him. Throughout the day he had freezing fits where he shook uncontrollably. His heart slugged against his ribs. The lung would work fine for a while and then his breathing would grow ragged and come in bites and gasps where he couldn't get enough air.

He should've cut the car loose of it by now. The businessman and the hooker had seen it at the motel, but it was a long shot anyone had grabbed the license. The car owed him and he owed the car. You don't soup this kind of muscle and not use it. The dark energy inside it still wanted out. He knew he'd have use of it farther on down the line.

He called a real estate agent to put the house up for sale. She showed up the next day and walked around the property, took measurements of the rooms and made lots of notes on her clipboard. They settled on a starting price, which was higher than Chase had expected.

Somebody finally got worried about Mrs. Nicholson and went over there and called the cops. It blew wide. The prowl cars stacked up in the road and the police canvassed the area. They came to his door and asked him questions about the Nicholsons. Animal control came along later that day with just as many vehicles as the cops had. It took four guys twenty minutes to round up all the cats.

The police wouldn't be able to cross all the T's but they'd have enough to satisfy them. They'd find out what Timmy Rosso's real name was and discover he was just a bartender posing as a criminal. They'd figure correctly he was double-crossed by wiser minds. There wouldn't be a high premium on the old lady and her retarded son.

In the morning, Morgan showed up at Chase's front door. He stared into Chase's eyes for a while and noted the bandages and the cast and said, "You look like shit."

"Feel that way too."

Staring some more, the hard-ass cop in Morgan wanted the entire truth, but didn't want it that badly. He'd already figured most of it out anyhow.

•

How could he not? It was more or less a straight line from his own desk to the motel.

Morgan nodded at the FOR SALE sign on the lawn. "You leaving?"

"Yeah."

"Soon?"

"Yeah."

"Good. Get the fuck out of here. Go far away. I don't ever want to see you again."

"You won't," Chase said.

You moved into the night and the night moved into you.

Chase showed up at the Deuce's chop shop. "That don's son. He still need someone who can drive?"

"Yeah," Deucie said, "but things are really ugly over there. I was an asshole to mention it to you in the first place. Infighting, mob-war bullshit. Between different families, in the same family, between New York and Jersey and Chicago, and the feds up everybody's ass with a microscope. A lot of bodies are turning up in the East River, or not at all. They're icing each other in restaurants, on street corners, wiping out girlfriends and kids like in the bad old days."

"Make the call."

Chewing the end of his cigar, Deucie frowned and stood there for a minute studying Chase. Then he let out a sigh of defeat and ran off to do it. Chase climbed back into the Chevelle and shut his eyes, the engine humming, crooning a love song to him.

The house was gone. Lila was buried twelve hundred miles away. He thought of Jonah out there, maybe with his baby girl and maybe not. The thought of the girl growing up in the life, following Jonah's lead, as bent as him, made Chase's stomach tighten. Sweat swarmed his back, but he was still too weak.

He figured there couldn't be that many professional surfers in Sarasota with wives named Milagro, who they called Milly. He could find the kid one way or another, his two-year-old aunt Kylie. He'd track her eventually, when he had a choice to offer her. Jonah had been right about one thing. Blood was important.

Chase had questions. He wanted to know why his father had said that he'd asked to make an appeal to the killer, when the truth was the cops had backed him into doing it. Chase wanted to know why his mother had cried so much right before she died.

The dream returned in full force. His unborn sibling tugging at his hand, Chase listening intently to the child, who knew the answers. A couple lines repeating themselves.

Angie had said, *Everyone else he destroys. More than you know.*

Jonah had said someone else had tried to kill him over a kid.

Another foolish woman.

Chase couldn't shake those words. They hummed and buzzed and bit at him.

He thought, Did Jonah murder my pregnant mother?

Waving a scrap of paper, Deuce returned and tried once more to talk Chase out of the job. Chase checked the name and address and said good-bye.

He cruised out of the shop and hit the street. He didn't feel any fear or hope or excitement. Just a nagging curiosity about his own past that would sharpen within him and drive him forward into another, perhaps a more decisive, confrontation with Jonah. Chase had shifted gears again, and now his life was on a different road. He still had things to do. Soothing music on the radio promised escape and intimacy as he drove on into the darkness thinking, Here it is. Here I am.

Look for Chase's return in

THE COLDEST MILE

by

Tom Piccirilli

Coming from

Bantam Books in 2009

About the Author

TOM PICCIRILLI lives in Colorado, where, besides writing, he spends an inordinate amount of time watching trash cult films and reading Gold Medal classic noir and hardboiled novels. He's a fan of Asian cinema, especially horror movies, bullet ballet, pinky violence, and samurai flicks. He also likes walking his dogs around the neighborhood. Are you starting to get the hint that he doesn't have a particularly active social life? Well, to heck with you, buddy, yours isn't much better. Give him any static and he'll smack you in the mush, dig? Tom also enjoys making new friends. He's the author of twenty novels, including *The Midnight Road*, *The Dead Letters*, *Headstone City*, *November Mourns*, and *A Choir of Ill Children*. He's a four-time winner of the Bram Stoker Award and a final nominee for the World Fantasy Award, the International Thriller Writers Award, and Le Grand Prix de L'Imaginaire. To learn more, check out his official website, Epitaphs, at www.tompiccirilli.com.

DON'T MISS

SPECTRA PULSE

A WORLD APART

the free monthly electronic newsletter
that delivers direct to you...

< Interviews with favorite authors
< Profiles of the hottest new writers
< Insider essays from Spectra's editorial
  team
< Chances to win free early copies of
  Spectra's new releases
< A peek at what's coming soon

...and so much more

SUBSCRIBE FREE TODAY AT

www.bantamdell.com

SF 2008